Amelia told herse~~~~~~~~~~~~~~~~~~~~~~~~~~~~~
crime deserved harsh ~~~~~~~~~~~ Still, this young man
intrigued her. She wondered why he'd ridden with the
notorious Nightriders gang.

Was it the excitement? The money? The danger?
Disrespect for the law?

Certainly only someone who held no respect for the
law would dare break it. Although Jesse Lawton didn't
appear to be disrespectful, she figured prison could beat
respect into a mangy dog.

But another reason for his unexpected politeness at
the depot nagged at her. Perhaps someone had made a
mistake. Perhaps Jesse Lawton was truly innocent.

The outlaw sliced his gaze over to her, and trepidation
slithered through her. He didn't look at all innocent.

He looked downright dangerous.

Amelia
and the
Outlaw

AN AVON TRUE ROMANCE

Amelia
and the
Outlaw

LORRAINE HEATH

AVON BOOKS
An Imprint of HarperCollinsPublishers

FIND TRUE LOVE!
www.avontrueromance.com

For Aunt Tack

with love

Amelia
and the
Outlaw

CHAPTER ONE

Fort Worth, Texas
May 1881

The first thing Jesse Lawton noticed when the train pulled into the station was the girl standing on the platform.

She was the prettiest thing he'd seen in five years.

Her blond hair was tucked up neatly beneath a frilly bonnet decorated with ribbons and bows. The tiny tips of her black leather shoes peeked out from beneath the hem of her spring-green dress.

He thought her eyes were blue, but he couldn't be certain—not from this distance, not peering through the dirty train window.

The girl jutted her bottom lip into a little pout that caused his insides to tighten. Her mouth reminded him of the plump strawberries he'd tasted at the beginning of a long-ago summer. He'd snitched them out of a garden that grew beside a house with gingham curtains fluttering in the windows and a white picket fence.

He'd convinced himself the pain in his gut was a result of being hungry—not the longing for all the comforts the folks inside the house took for granted. He'd forced himself to gobble down the juicy berries and not think about soft beds or clean clothes or a warm bath.

The girl rocked back and forth on her heels, twirling her little green reticule as if she were waiting on somebody.

He couldn't take his eyes off her—which was a blessing. Looking at her prevented him from having to acknowledge the stares of the passengers making their way off the train. He kept his hands tucked between his thighs, so the shackles on his wrists weren't quite as visible.

But people noticed them anyway. He could tell when they did, because he'd hear them gasp or whisper harshly to their traveling companion that a criminal had been sitting in their midst.

"Hey, mister, are you an outlaw?" a boy suddenly asked loudly.

Flinching inwardly, Jesse focused his attention more intently on the girl. She was tapping her foot now, her growing impatience apparent.

"Run along, son," the man sitting beside him said.

Jesse didn't know his name. His guard hadn't bothered with introductions when he'd slapped on the irons.

"Is he an outlaw?" the kid asked again, his excitement

echoing around the small compartment. "Is he?"

"Used to be," the man said. "Ain't no more. Now he's a prisoner of the state."

Jesse felt as though he'd been a prisoner of the state for most of his life. His mother had left him on somebody's doorstep, wrapped in a tattered blanket with a note that simply said, *Please love him.*

No one had bothered to comply with her request. He'd been passed around from person to person, never feeling as though anyone truly wanted him. At least not until he'd joined up with the Nightriders gang. Under the leadership of Sometimes-One-Eyed Pete, for a time, at least, he'd thought he'd discovered where he belonged.

But the bungled bank robbery had found him sentenced to spend ten years at Huntsville Prison. He'd already survived five in that wretched hole. Now he had a chance to serve his remaining time beneath the blue Texas sky. He didn't intend to lose this opportunity—no matter what the cost.

The guard stood. "Let's go, boy."

Jesse unfolded his body, moved into the aisle, and headed for the door. The guard trailed behind him with his rifle held at the ready in the crook of his arm. Jesse knew the man would just as soon shoot him as see him get off the train, so he kept his strides short, slow, nonthreatening.

He walked through the door and to the steps that led to the platform. Placing one hand on the railing forced him to put both there because of the way his hands were linked together. He climbed down carefully, awkwardly.

He didn't dare look for the pretty girl now. He prayed she'd moved on and wouldn't catch sight of him with the humiliating chains jangling between his wrists.

With the butt of his rifle, the guard shoved him forward. "Keep going. Judge Harper is standing right over there."

Even if the guard hadn't pointed him out, Jesse would have recognized Judge Harper. He'd lost track of the number of days that had passed since he'd been escorted to the warden's office, where he'd met the judge for the first time.

Judge Harper had only recently replaced Judge Gray, better known as the Hanging Judge—the man who had sentenced Jesse to ten years of hard time. Jesse hadn't been able to work up a spark of pity when word had traveled through the prison that the Hanging Judge had met his maker.

Judge Harper had been reviewing Judge Gray's records. Apparently the previous judge had kept detailed accounts on every criminal who'd appeared in his courtroom and every sentence he'd handed down.

"I don't like doubting my predecessor," Judge Harper had said, "but I think he might have been a bit harsh when he sentenced you."

A bit harsh? Jesse thought that was an understatement. The man had been downright mean, with a steely glare that had made Jesse fear the Hanging Judge was going to live up to his reputation and sentence Jesse to dance in the wind from the nearest oak tree.

"I'm not willing to commute your sentence," Judge Harper continued, "but I'm willing to let you serve out your time under less desolate conditions."

So here Jesse was, his mouth suddenly as dry as a west Texas wind, walking toward the man who held his freedom in his hands. Judge Harper had looked imposing and ominous when he'd met with Jesse at Huntsville.

He was even more so now, standing on the platform in black trousers, a black jacket, and a black hat with his dark eyes roaming over Jesse, taking in every little detail of his existence. Jesse was nearly as tall as the judge, but held under his intense scrutiny, he felt remarkably smaller.

Judge Harper pressed his lips into a hard line of disapproval, and Jesse figured he was going to be getting right back on the train and heading toward Huntsville before the sun set.

"Did he give you trouble?" Judge Harper asked.

"No, sir," the guard said. "I just wasn't willing to take any chances with a convict."

Judge Harper narrowed his eyes, and Jesse wondered if the man was striving to search his soul.

"Are you planning to cause any trouble?" Judge Harper asked.

"No, sir," Jesse answered.

The judge nodded. "Get the shackles off him."

"With all due respect, Judge, if he was to escape—"

"My boys will track him down," Judge Harper interrupted.

Jesse noticed the two men standing on either side of the judge. With their dark hair and similar stances, they looked enough like Judge Harper that he figured they were his sons.

"And he'll regret the day he was born," Judge Harper finished.

Jesse didn't figure the judge or his sons could make him regret that day any more than he already did.

He cringed when the guard inserted the key into the lock and the grinding of metal echoed around him. Anyone who hadn't noticed his chains before was sure to notice them now. He suspected the guard deliberately made as much commotion as possible.

As soon as the shackles fell away, Jesse dropped his arms to his sides, refusing to rub his aching wrists and give his guard any satisfaction from knowing the discomfort he'd caused. He fought to hold the judge's gaze when he desperately wanted to look away.

"Thanks, Thaddeus, you can go now," the judge said to the guard.

"But if he escapes—"

"Are you going to try to escape?" Judge Harper asked.

"No, sir."

They had a deal, and although the judge had no reason to believe otherwise, Jesse had never broken his word. Broken the law, yes, but never gone back on his word.

The judge nodded, and Jesse almost thought he saw a softening in those dark eyes. "That'll be all, Thaddeus."

"Yes, sir."

Leaning near Jesse, the guard whispered in a low voice, "Keep your nose clean, boy. You don't want to end up back in my prison."

If that wasn't the gosh-darned truth, Jesse didn't know what was. After the guard climbed back on the train, some of Jesse's tension eased away.

The judge gave Jesse another slow perusal before saying, "These are my sons. Robert and David."

Both men gave him a nod. Neither dared to lie and say he was pleased to meet Jesse. They appeared to be a little older than Jesse's nineteen years.

"We've got several things to discuss," Judge Harper said, "but we can do it back at the ranch. The wagon's over here. Amelia?"

At the click of approaching footsteps, Jesse turned his head . . . and there she was, the pretty girl he'd been staring at while he'd sat on the train. His stomach dropped clear down to his boots. She'd seen him clamber down the steps, heard the awful clang of his shackles, and had to know of his crimes.

"This is my daughter, Amelia," the judge said.

Up close she was even lovelier than she'd appeared from a distance. Her eyes were green, not blue. Green like a patch of clover he'd once napped in.

He snatched his hat from his head and crushed the brim with his hands.

"Ma'am." His voice sounded as though he hadn't used it in at least a dozen years.

Her eyes twinkled and her lips curled up slightly. "It's a pleasure to meet you, Mr. Lawton."

Unlike her brothers, she apparently had no qualms about stretching the truth, although he had a difficult time believing a voice as lyrical as hers could ever utter a lie. She was a dainty little thing, but she also gave off an air of confidence that came from knowing she belonged.

"I didn't much like that guard," she said. "He seemed mean-spirited."

Jesse stared at her. He'd never heard anyone except fellow prisoners say something unflattering about a guard.

"It's his job to be harsh," David Harper said. "Otherwise convicts would be escaping all over the place."

"Papa's harsh," she said. "But he's not mean. There's a difference. Don't you agree, Mr. Lawton?"

Jesse couldn't think of a single thing to say as she held his gaze.

"Cat got your tongue?" she asked.

"That'll be enough now, Amelia," Judge Harper said.

"You see," she said. "Harsh but not mean."

Her mouth blossomed into a smile that stole his breath as surely as he'd stolen money from a half dozen banks. He wanted to tuck that smile into his pocket so he could take it out and look at it from time to time.

The judge cleared his throat, and Jesse dropped his gaze to his well-worn boots. He figured if the judge thought he had an interest in his daughter, he'd put him right back on the train.

And that wouldn't do at all. The last place Jesse ever wanted to go again was prison.

As the wagon rumbled over the dirt road, Amelia Harper sat on the bench seat beside her father while her brothers huddled in the back with the outlaw.

The outlaw.

Jesse Lawton certainly didn't look like a criminal to her. His cheeks had actually flushed when he'd removed his hat upon being introduced to her. She'd never seen a man blush before, and she'd spent time around a lot of men: her father, her brothers, and all the cowboys who worked her father's ranch.

But it was the outlaw's blue eyes that had captured

and held her attention. Weary. As though he'd seen too much of life and didn't care to see much more.

"Papa, how old did you say Jesse was?" she asked quietly, hoping the squeaking of the wagon and the clip-clop of the horses' hooves would keep her voice from traveling to the outlaw's ears.

"Nineteen," her father said in an equally low voice.

"He looks older than Robert's twenty-four years," she said.

"He's had a hard life. Judge Gray didn't make it any easier." He looked askance at her. "You're not to flirt with him. He's not one of the cowhands you can wrap around your finger."

Jesse had furrows in his brow, as though he worried often. He had no laugh lines around his mouth to indicate he ever smiled. Although she could well imagine he had little to smile about.

"I simply wanted to reassure him that your bark is worse than your bite," she explained.

"Until I get a true measure of the young man," her father said quietly, "let's let him think my bite is something to worry about."

Most people did see her father as gruff and uncompromising. She knew it was just his way. But sometimes he could be downright intimidating.

She stared straight ahead, picturing in her mind her first impressions of the outlaw.

Her brothers were dressed much as her father was: neatly pressed white shirt, black jacket, black string tie, and black trousers. They represented with no mistake exactly what they were: the successful sons of a successful man.

Jesse Lawton, on the other hand, looked as though he was a complete stranger to success.

His clothes were bedraggled, giving the impression that someone had scrounged them out of the bottom of an abandoned box. Amelia thought the state was supposed to provide released prisoners with new clothes, but then Jesse Lawton wasn't truly being set free.

His britches were worn, his boots even more so. His hat looked as though it had been stuffed into a trunk somewhere. It suddenly occurred to her that it probably had been. She didn't think they let prisoners hold on to their personal possessions.

His hair—the black of a moonless night—was in desperate need of trimming. She was surprised to discover she had a desire to cut it, and more, she wanted to take a razor to the bristles shadowing his face. But she didn't think either action would soften the ruggedness that seemed to be such a part of him.

Almost as tall as her father and Robert, a little taller than David, he had wide shoulders and a broad chest that spoke of hard labor. Yet he also possessed a wiriness that reminded her of a starving coyote she'd once seen attack the herd. His clothes fairly hung off his body as though no one had bothered to measure him before replacing his prison uniform with an outfit that would prevent him from standing out in the crowd.

Still, he had stood out. Not so much because of the awful shackles he'd been wearing, but because of the wariness that emanated from him. As though he didn't expect trust and wouldn't be disappointed if he didn't receive it.

She imagined prison life wasn't easy.

As a matter of fact, its very harshness had haunted her father when he'd discovered that Judge Gray had sent a fourteen-year-old boy to prison. Two weeks ago her father called a family meeting to discuss his plan to put a convicted man within their midst—before he'd approached Jesse Lawton with his offer.

He could serve his remaining five years under the judge's supervision, working at his ranch. The labor would be as hard as or harder than the work he did in prison, but as long as he didn't cause trouble he'd have a semblance of freedom. In five years' time, he could go or stay. The choice would be his.

Amelia imagined he'd hightail it to the far corners of the state faster than a cat with its tail on fire. Not that she could blame him. She knew a little about not having freedom.

Ten days shy of seventeen, she thought she was old

enough to make her own decisions, but her father seldom agreed. Since her mother had passed away when Amelia was twelve, Amelia had no other parent to appeal to. Her father's words were the law of the family. Some principles he simply wouldn't compromise.

Amelia wanted to wear britches when she rode around the ranch. He insisted she wear a split skirt.

She wanted to read dime novels; he insisted she read Shakespeare.

She wanted a beau. He forbade her from having gentlemen callers until her birthday—as though ten more days made a world of difference between her being a girl and a young woman.

Sighing with frustration at the reminder of her limitations, Amelia shifted her gaze back toward her father. She loved him dearly. She only wished he'd grant her as much freedom as he planned to give this outlaw. But her father was in the habit of laying down rules and having them obeyed unconditionally.

She'd overheard him tell the outlaw that they had things to discuss. She knew just what he'd say in his resonant, booming voice: Don't do this and don't do that.

He'd used the same tone when he'd explained she was to never, ever put herself in a situation that would leave her alone with Jesse Lawton. She knew it was simply her father's way, to issue orders like some general commanding troops. Probably a habit he'd developed during the

War Between the States when he *had* commanded troops. Still, she resented all the rules and the fact that she had to find ways around them in order to have any fun.

Finding a way around his order to steer clear of Jesse would be a real challenge. She understood her father's precaution regarding the outlaw. She truly did, but she'd never been around anyone who'd broken the law, anyone who'd been sent to prison. Jesse fascinated her as much as the law did.

While her father had been establishing his ranch, he'd also worked as a lawyer in Fort Worth. He'd watched the town change from a military outpost into one of the most prosperous and progressive cities in the state. Lawyers had benefited from its rapid growth. Amelia had often listened to her father explaining various aspects of the law to her brothers. She'd even questioned him about some matters, wanting more information than he provided.

He'd answered her questions with an indulgent smile. Then he'd say, "It's a shame you're not a boy. You have a sharp mind and more interest in the law than your brothers."

She didn't think it was a *shame* that she was a girl. She simply thought it was unfair that people thought girls should be interested only in taking care of a house, getting married, and raising children. Amelia was interested in so much more.

She was contemplating becoming a lawyer. She'd even begun studying her father's law books.

She also welcomed the idea of perhaps following in her father's footsteps and eventually becoming a judge. But she couldn't help but wonder if she had it within her to sentence a man to prison. To take away his freedom when she so valued hers.

Out of the corner of her eye, she could see Jesse. With one leg stretched out, he dangled a scarred wrist across the knee he'd raised.

She didn't want to think about the shackles he'd been wearing when he'd clambered off the train, or how many times before today he might have been forced to wear them. They'd sounded heavy when the guard had removed them. Heavy and uncomfortable.

She told herself that anyone who committed a crime deserved harsh treatment. Still, this young man intrigued her. She wondered why he'd ridden with the notorious Nightriders gang.

Was it the excitement? The money? The danger? Disrespect for the law?

Certainly only someone who held no respect for the law would dare break it. Although Jesse Lawton didn't appear to be disrespectful, she figured prison could beat respect into a mangy dog.

But another reason for his unexpected politeness at the depot nagged at her. Perhaps someone had made a mistake. Perhaps Jesse Lawton was truly innocent.

The outlaw sliced his gaze over to her, and trepidation slithered through her. He didn't look at all innocent.

He looked downright dangerous.

CHAPTER TWO

Twilight was easing over the land by the time the judge pulled the wagon to a halt in front of a large brick house. It stood two stories tall, larger than anything Jesse had ever seen. A huge porch supported by white columns welcomed visitors.

A man with hair the color of a muddy river sat on the porch. He slowly came to his feet as everyone climbed out of the wagon.

Jesse's feet hit the dirt path, sending up a plume of dust. For a moment he stood mesmerized, watching as the judge helped his daughter. She placed her delicate hands on his shoulders while he wrapped his around her waist. He lifted her down as though she weighed no more than a wispy cloud.

Jesse had caught her watching him several times during the journey. Every time he'd given her a hard glare, expecting her to look away. Instead she'd defiantly held his gaze, tilting up that cute chin of hers until *he'd* finally looked away, embarrassed that she knew where he'd spent the last five years of his life.

The man who'd been sitting on the porch approached. "Judge."

The judge gave him a curt nod before turning to Jesse. "Jesse, this is Tanner, my foreman."

The wind and sun had practically turned Tanner's face into leather, but his gray eyes held kindness. He stuck out his hand. "Welcome to the Lazy H, but you'll discover soon enough that we're anything but lazy around here."

Jesse wasn't exactly sure what to do. He'd seen the gesture a thousand times as he'd ridden through towns, whenever men on the boardwalk stopped to talk to those they knew. But he'd never placed his hand in another's.

He could feel Amelia watching him, studying him, as the seconds ticked by and his unease with the situation grew.

"The custom of shaking a hand in greeting was started during the medieval period," Amelia said softly, as though understanding his hesitation. "A knight extended his hand to show that he wasn't holding a weapon."

Jesse jerked his attention to her. "I don't have a gun."

"Of course you don't. I didn't mean that you did. I was just explaining—"

"An old wives' tale," David interrupted. "Just shake Tanner's hand."

With reluctance, Jesse wiped his sweating palm on his britches before taking Tanner's hand. Tanner gave Jesse's hand a quick shake and released his hold. Jesse didn't understand how that little action told a man that the other wasn't carrying a weapon. After all, a man had two hands.

"That wasn't so bad, was it?" Amelia asked.

Before Jesse could answer, the judge said, "I think we've done all the talking out here that we need to do. Let's get up to the house."

Jesse was hoping that order didn't include him, but when everyone else started up the steps, leaving him rooted in the dust, he had a feeling it did. He was torn between going inside and staying where he was.

He'd never been inside a house that looked like this one. Oh, for a while when he was small he'd lived with a widow who'd kept her house as clean as she'd kept him, scrubbing his body with the same brush she'd used for the floors.

But he'd never been inside a building that housed a family.

As uncomfortable as he felt about following them, he was equally curious and desperate to know what other people possessed.

"Jesse?"

Jesse jumped at the judge's insistent voice. The man waited in the doorway.

Jesse trudged up the steps and entered the house. The scent of flowers greeted him. He'd never been in a place that smelled like a field of wildflowers in spring. For the most part, when he'd stayed indoors before prison, he'd usually stayed in storage rooms or barns.

"We'll talk in my library," the judge said, indicating a room off to the side.

Jesse followed him inside and came to an abrupt halt. He'd never seen so many books in his entire life. They lined the shelves on two walls, from the floor to the ceiling. He wondered if the judge had read them all. He wondered even more how so many different stories could exist.

He shifted his attention to the judge's daughter. With her hands folded on her lap, she sat elegantly in a chair off to the side. Her gaze roamed over him in a leisurely fashion that caused the heat of embarrassment to build within him.

He'd never cared much about his appearance, but right now he felt as though every aspect of his person were sorely lacking. He watched her watching him, wondering if she would find anything about him that pleased her. Wondering more why he cared whether she did or not.

She seemed completely at ease here, as though she knew she was safe, knew she would always be so. She'd probably never had a day of sadness in her life. Strangely, he didn't envy her that fact. Rather he was glad.

He wouldn't wish his life on his worst enemy.

The judge cleared his throat, and Jesse snapped his attention around to the man wearing a scowl of disapproval. Obviously showing any interest at all in the judge's daughter was not a good idea.

The judge sat in a large leather chair behind a massive mahogany desk, presiding over the room as he no doubt did his courtroom. His sons propped themselves on either corner of the desk, like sentinels who thought it was their job to protect their father. With his arms crossed over his chest, Tanner stood behind the judge and off to the side, close to the fireplace.

To the right of Tanner, nestled in a corner, was a large safe. Jesse had opened a half dozen like it in his time. It was too large and heavy to be moved—probably the reason Judge Harper didn't bother to hide it. Its contents were well protected unless a man had dynamite or sensitive fingertips and sharp hearing. Jesse possessed the latter.

"I may own this land," Judge Harper began, once again capturing Jesse's attention, "but Tanner runs things for me. You'll take your orders from him. He's not going to cut you any slack. You disobey him once, and you'll find yourself back at Huntsville. Understand?"

So much for Jesse's hope that life here would be different from life in prison.

Still he answered, "Yes, sir."

"If my sons give you an order, you follow without question. Understand?"

"Yes, sir."

"You're to stay away from my daughter." Judge Harper practically sliced Jesse in two with his gaze. "Understand?"

Jesse fought not to shift his gaze over to Amelia. "Yes, sir."

Judge Harper sighed and leaned back in his chair. "You're free to move about the ranch as long as you let Tanner or my sons know where you're going. You don't tell them, and you're back at Huntsville. Understand?"

"Yes, sir."

"Try to escape and you're back at Huntsville. You'll notice I said 'try,' because I give you my word that my sons are fine trackers. Understand?"

Jesse was beginning to sound like an echo. "Yes, sir."

"No drinking, no gambling, no fighting, no cussing. Those are my rules. Break one of them, and you're back at Huntsville. Understand?"

He decided he'd be lucky to last through the night. Still, he nodded. "Yes, sir."

"All right, then, Tanner will take you to the bunkhouse and introduce you to the men. I have no tolerance for lawbreakers. I'm giving you a chance here to prove that Judge Gray's judgment regarding you was wrong. Don't squander this opportunity to better your life."

"Yes, sir."

Tanner uncrossed his arms, stepped away from his exalted position behind the judge, and rounded the desk. "Let's go."

Jesse wondered if he should say something to Judge Harper before leaving, but he couldn't think of anything that might be appropriate. The man's good intentions were welcome . . . even if they came with a lot of rules. But he couldn't quite bring himself to thank the man. As far as Jesse was concerned, one judge wasn't that much different from any other.

So Jesse simply nodded and fell into step behind the foreman as he walked out of the room. He was eager to get away from the judge's sons, who'd been boring their gazes into him as though they'd wanted to drill clear into his soul.

And he definitely wanted to get away from the judge's daughter, because *not* looking at her was about the hardest thing he'd ever done in his life.

As they stepped onto the porch, Jesse took comfort in the dimming twilight. It signaled one less day he had to serve for his crimes.

He followed Tanner as he headed toward a wood-framed building in the distance, past the barn. Jesse cast a longing glance at the horses prancing within the nearby corral. With one of them beneath him, he could hightail it—

"You know any other words besides 'yes, sir'?" Tanner asked, interrupting Jesse's thoughts of escape.

Jesse tore his gaze from the corral and focused it on the man walking beside him, walking as though he wasn't in any hurry to be anywhere.

"Yes, sir," he responded dryly.

Prison had taught him to say as little as possible in order to survive. Never tell a man more than he needed to know. Never reveal what the world couldn't see on its own.

Tanner didn't break his stride while he looked at Jesse as though measuring him. "I know Judge Harper seems like a hard man, but he's risked a lot bringing you here. His reputation, his business, his family. He has a right to set down rules. Perhaps even an obligation to do so."

Jesse was growing weary of the reminders that his freedom was only an illusion. They all worried about what it was costing the judge. No one seemed concerned with what it was costing him—to see all the things he'd never possessed. And never would.

He wasn't thinking about the fancy knickknacks that decorated the small tables or the pretty pictures hanging on the walls. He was thinking about the solidarity and familiarity that emanated from the folks in that room.

Everyone seemed secure in their place, knew where they belonged. Jesse couldn't imagine the satisfaction that might come from filling up the empty places in his soul with those emotions.

Tanner stopped short of the bunkhouse door. "I'll be honest with you, Jesse. A lot of the men aren't comfortable with the idea of having you around. You just steer clear of them, and I don't think we'll have any problems."

Jesse narrowed his eyes. One more rule to follow.

"Me, I think every man deserves a second chance, but I'll be watching you closely," Tanner continued. "Like Judge Harper said, disobey one of his rules and you'll find yourself back at Huntsville."

Jesse heard a cacophony of sounds emanating from inside the bunkhouse: deep voices, laughter, the scraping of chairs over a floor, and footsteps. He didn't much welcome the prospect of facing a new bunch of strangers, but his whole life had been filled with nothing but strangers. He should have been accustomed to it by now, but his stomach knotted up, his mouth grew dry, and his palms got sweaty.

He swallowed hard and fought not to show his apprehension. "You gonna jaw all night or get on with this?"

A corner of Tanner's mouth tilted up. "Reckon I'll get on with it. If you have any problems, though, you come see me."

Right. Jesse was certain that somewhere in both the judge's and Tanner's words resided the unspoken warning that if he complained he'd be back at Huntsville. He understood that fact without its being said directly.

Tanner opened the door and stepped inside. Jesse followed. A hush fell over the room. The fellas who were playing poker at a table no longer looked at the cards they held in their hands. Instead they narrowed their eyes and stared at Jesse.

Men who'd been lying in bunks slowly sat up as though to challenge him.

"This here's Jesse, the new hand Judge Harper spoke to you about," Tanner announced, his voice booming to the distant corners. "I don't want any trouble, Jesse doesn't want any trouble, and I guarantee the judge doesn't want any. If you've got any problems with this situation, you come see me."

Tanner jerked his head to the side. "That'll be your bed. Far corner, upper bunk."

Jesse gave a curt nod before wending his way among tables, chairs, and outstretched legs. He met the gaze of every man who dared him to look away. He'd learned in prison never to show fear even if he was quaking in his boots. Survival depended on being the first one to set up defenses.

The fella sitting on the lower bed below Jesse's slowly stood, his fists bunched at his sides, his eyes never straying from Jesse.

Ignoring him, Jesse planted his foot on the bottom bed and hoisted himself onto the bed up top. Stretching out, he folded his arms beneath his head and stared at the knotholes in the ceiling.

He'd done a quick tally and counted ten double bunks, so he figured the ranch probably had close to twenty workers. He felt distrust and hatred emanating from each one of them. The hard truth hit him painfully.

Living here wasn't going to be much different from being in prison after all.

CHAPTER THREE

"Amelia, stop picking at your food," her father ordered.

When in the world is he going to stop treating me like a child and allow me to do as I please? If I'm not in the mood to eat, why do I have to eat?

Turning her attention away from the slice of lamb resting on her plate that she'd been poking with her fork, Amelia met her father's gaze where he sat at the head of the table. Robert and David sat on either side of him. She had the dubious honor of sitting beside David.

"I can't seem to stop thinking about that outlaw," she admitted. She'd felt sorry for him, standing in front of her father as he'd listed the conditions under which Jesse could stay at the ranch.

"He won't hurt you," her father assured her.

"I'm not afraid of him," she said. At least, she didn't want to be afraid of him. "I was just wondering if it was really necessary to give him so many rules to follow."

"I simply didn't want any misunderstandings to arise," he stated flatly.

She didn't think there was much chance of that

happening. Her father was a man governed by the law, but sometimes she thought he took his dedication to it to the extreme.

"Why do you think he did it?" Amelia asked. "Robbed the bank, I mean."

"A lazy man looking for easy money," Robert said.

"Only he wasn't a *man*," she pointed out. "He was still a boy, a child really."

"Fourteen is old enough to be considered a man," David said. "We've had cowboys who weren't much older than that working for us when we've driven cattle north."

She truly wasn't interested in her brothers' opinions. They didn't know any more about Jesse Lawton than she did. Her father, on the other hand, had read Judge Gray's account of the case.

"Papa, why do you think he did it?" she repeated.

"I suspect Robert hit the nail on the head. The boy was looking for an easy way out."

"Prison doesn't seem like an easy way to me," she told him.

"He didn't plan on getting caught, Amelia," David said, as though she didn't possess a lick of sense.

Sometimes her brothers were an irritating nuisance. Just because they were older didn't mean they were smarter.

She moved her carrots from one side of her plate to the other. Watching Jesse get off the train, she'd felt a whole range of emotions. She'd originally been frightened at the sight of his shackles, thinking he must be dangerous if he had to be restrained.

But as she'd approached him and seen the loneliness in his eyes, she'd felt a strong urge to comfort him. Until he'd given her a look from the back of the wagon that had reminded her of a hungry wolf. Strangely, rather than making her wary, he'd only served to pique her curiosity and to confuse her.

"I thought he'd look mean," she murmured.

How did Jesse manage to look dangerous without appearing to be terrifying? She'd always associated fear with danger. But what she felt now wasn't a scary sensation, but more of an exciting allure.

"Don't be fooled, Amelia," Robert said. "Judge Gray didn't send him to prison without good reason."

She gnawed on her lower lip. "If Papa believed that, he wouldn't have brought Jesse here." She turned to her father. "You think Judge Gray was wrong, don't you?"

Her father sighed. "I don't know. I don't like second-guessing another judge. Jesse was involved in an armed bank robbery during a time when crime in Fort Worth was escalating. A man was shot. He didn't die, but he came close. I suppose Judge Gray wanted to make an example of Jesse. I don't fault him for that. I just thought the sentence seemed a bit harsh for a fourteen-year-old."

"For all we know, maybe it wasn't harsh enough," David said. "I just hope we don't all come to regret your good intentions."

Her father shoved his plate away, as though by doing so he could bring an end to the conversation. "Until we can get a good measure of the young man, I want you to watch him closely, but give him some slack."

"He'll just hang himself with it," Robert said.

Her brothers usually weren't negative, but then they normally didn't have an outlaw walking among them.

"It'll be his choice if he does," her father said.

"What do you know about him?" Amelia asked. "Other than the fact that he's an outlaw, I mean."

"Not much," her father admitted. "Judge Gray wrote more about the crime than he did the offender."

"Jesse seems polite enough," she offered.

"I reckon prison can beat politeness into you," David said.

Amelia hated to admit she'd thought the same thing earlier. It wasn't often she and David agreed on anything—except for their enjoyment of dime novels. He had so many books that she could always snitch one out of his bedroom without his noticing.

Her father shook his head slightly, furrowing his brow. "He was short on words, but polite when I visited him in prison. That's the reason I decided it was safe to take a chance and let him serve out his time here." He pointed his finger toward her. "But you, young lady, are to stay away from him."

Amelia decided that task would be easier said than done. She was fascinated with the outlaw and his deep blue eyes that reflected a sadness she didn't think she could even begin to imagine.

Since entering the bunkhouse, Jesse hadn't spoken a single word to anyone, and no one had spoken to him. The cowhand who slept in the bunk beneath his had finally returned to his bed when he realized Jesse wasn't going to fight him.

Shortly after eight o'clock, Tanner had announced it was time to hit the sack. Cards had been put away and lanterns dimmed before most of the men had crawled onto their beds.

Some snored. Jesse was able to block out the noise, though. Men had snored in prison. Other prisoners had sobbed or yelled out in their sleep. Prison was never quiet, never still. There was always a sound, a restless movement, a wanting to be somewhere else so badly. . . .

And right now he wanted to be anywhere but here. He shifted his gaze from the shadows dancing across the ceiling to those washing over the door. Moonlight eased in through the slats of the shutters covering the windows. Not a lot of light, but enough that he could see that no one sat in chairs near the tables or windows.

Tanner had left the bunkhouse after shouting another order for everyone to be quiet and get some shut-eye. He hadn't returned. The temptation to step outside overwhelmed Jesse.

It had been a little over five years since he'd been able to leave a room simply because he wanted to.

The bed moaned as he sat up and swung his legs over the side of the bunk. He held his breath, waiting for someone to tell him to lie back down.

But no such order came. And it dawned on him that he didn't have to answer to these men. He only had to report to Tanner, and he wasn't around.

Carefully, quietly, he eased off the bunk until his boots touched the ground with a hushed thud. He considered removing them, but where he wanted to go, he'd need them. Besides, removing them would probably make more noise than just creeping to the door.

So he crept. He heard someone stir and someone else snort. A muffled cough. A squeaking bed.

But no one came forward to stop him.

The hinges creaked as he opened the door slightly and slipped into the night.

He drew in a deep breath of clean air. He didn't know if anything had ever smelled so sweet.

"Going somewhere?" a deep voice asked, nearly sending him leaping off the porch.

He twisted around. In the shadows beneath the

eaves, he made out Tanner's silhouette.

"I needed some air," he said defensively.

"Yeah, I know that feeling. Some of those boys don't wash their socks often enough."

It wasn't the smell of feet or sweat or bodies that had caused him to want to leave. It was everything closing in on him . . . getting smaller and smaller until it was no bigger than a closet.

"You always guard the door?" Jesse asked, resentment rising in him like burning bile. He knew he had no reason to be trusted, but he hated having every movement watched and measured. When the judge had made his offer, Jesse had thought he was getting out of prison. Instead he was discovering that it had simply taken on a different shape.

"I always take some time in the evening to relax out here before I turn in," Tanner said. "You got a problem with my habits?"

"No, sir."

Jesse glanced toward the corral. He needed to walk somewhere, to escape for a few minutes, to pretend he wasn't shackled by his past crimes.

"Can I take a walk around here?" he asked.

"I'm not your jailer, boy."

He snapped his head around. "I thought you were."

"I'm supposed to keep an eye on you, but I don't plan to watch you like a hawk. I give you my word, though, that if you run off, I'll hunt you down if the Harper boys don't find you first."

"I've got no plans to run off. As bad as this is, it's a lot better than prison."

"I know that for a fact," Tanner said.

Jesse's breath caught. "You've been to prison?"

"My past is my business. Take your walk."

With a deep breath, Jesse stepped off the porch and headed for the corral. In prison, his job had been to tend to the needs of the guards' horses: brushing them, feeding them, and keeping their stalls clean. His desire to get close to the familiar was almost overwhelming.

He'd enjoyed caring for the animals. He wasn't certain what his chores around here would entail, but maybe he could look out for the animals as well.

He glanced toward the house. Pale light spilled out of a couple of the windows on the second floor. He wondered if any of the windows visible to him belonged to Amelia. It would be a lot easier serving out his time here if she weren't around.

In the judge's library, he'd been torn between wanting to look at her and being ashamed that he'd ever been sent to prison.

He reached the corral and folded his arms over the top railing. Several paddocks fanned out from this one. The others housed several horses each, but within this main one, a lone horse cantered around the edge of the fence as though it felt as restless as Jesse did. As though it, too, wanted to escape. Moonlight played over its shiny black coat.

Jesse clicked his tongue behind his teeth, making a little clacking sound as he held out his hand.

"Come here," he said softly. "Come here."

He'd always drawn comfort from the animals he'd tended. They didn't judge a man even when he deserved judgment.

The horse cautiously approached. Jesse reached out and rubbed its muzzle. He wished he had a bit of an apple or a carrot to offer.

"She bites," a soft feminine voice said.

Jesse snatched his hand back and spun around. The judge's daughter stood beside him, her hair no longer piled on her head, but draped over one shoulder in a long braid.

He shoved his hands into his britches pockets and took a step back. He was near enough that he could smell her honeysuckle scent.

"Cat got your tongue?" she asked.

She'd asked him the same thing at the depot, and he hadn't known what to say then either. His mouth felt dry enough that it was possible something had hold of his tongue. He'd been fourteen the last time he'd actually spoken to a female beyond the introductions. He couldn't even recall the girl's name now. Her father had owned the general store in the last town he'd ridden through before the botched bank robbery.

Behind the general store, he'd kissed her more than he'd talked to her. She'd been a little wild, had sensed the danger in him, and had been lured by it. Or so she'd whispered in between kisses.

But now he wasn't nearly as dangerous as the girl who stood before him. All she had to do was snap her fingers, and he'd be back behind prison walls.

"I'm supposed to stay away from you." He sounded breathless, as though he'd run out to the corral.

"So go on back to the bunkhouse if you're scared."

His pride bristled at her challenge. "I'm not scared."

But he was. He didn't want to go back to prison, and staying away from her was a rule. He pointed toward the bunkhouse. "Tanner's sitting on the porch."

"Knowing Tanner, he won't interfere unless I holler. He believes in giving a person more freedom than my father does."

Still, Tanner was watching, and all he had to do was tell the judge that Jesse had been out here with Amelia and he'd be back at prison. He knew he should leave, but he didn't want her thinking he was afraid. He'd learned in prison that to survive he couldn't let anyone know he was afraid.

So he stayed, with his stomach knotting up and his

blood thundering in his ears.

She turned away from him, stepped on the bottom rung of the fence, and crossed her arms over the top railing. The horse neared, and Amelia held out her hand.

Even in the darkness, Jesse could tell she had something in her palm. He saw the horse nudge her hand and then heard the crisp echo of munching.

"Thought you said she bites," he said, irritated that her earlier comment had caused him to snatch his hand back.

"She's not silly enough to bite the hand that feeds her. Are you?"

"What do you mean?"

She turned her head toward him, and he saw the moonlight dancing in her eyes and outlining the curves of her cheeks.

"You look at my father as though you resent him."

"I resent the rules," he admitted.

"I'm not too fond of them myself," she said.

Jesse knew he should head back to the bunkhouse, but his chest ached with wanting. For just a few minutes, if he kept his distance, maybe no harm would come from pretending that he was like every other fella in the bunkhouse—was truly free to pursue his dreams.

He glanced over his shoulder. No sign of Tanner.

Maybe he could stay a minute more.

Amelia pulled her hand out of her pocket and handed another morsel of apple to the horse. "Don't you think she's beautiful?" she asked.

He couldn't remember the last time anyone had asked his opinion on a matter. Why would she care what he thought about her horse? "Maybe," he answered.

"You're not much of a talker, are you?"

"I talk when I've got something to say."

"Which apparently isn't very often. Aren't you curious about my horse?"

He could imagine Tanner watching him, counting off the minutes. "I need to get back to the bunkhouse."

"We've had Duchess for almost two months," she said quickly, "but no one has been able to break her. Papa says you worked with the prison's horses."

"So?" he asked, irritated that she knew his private business. Although he supposed as a prisoner, he really had no private business.

"Do you know much about horses?"

"Some."

"If she's not broken soon, he'll get rid of her. He doesn't have much tolerance for rebellion—in animals or people."

He thought he detected a measure of resentment in her voice. He couldn't imagine that she did much rebelling, although he had to admit she was out here in the dead of night talking to him.

"Duchess," she said softly, sending a shiver racing through him from his chin to his toes. He envied the horse because she was rubbing its nose. "Why won't you let anyone break you?"

"Some horses aren't meant to be broken," Jesse said.

"But she's supposed to be my birthday present." She leaned over and kissed the horse's forehead. "I want to ride her, but I'm forbidden to even try until one of the men can ride her without being tossed."

"And you always do what you're told," he guessed.

"Obviously not. I'm out here talking to you, aren't I?"

"You're talking to your horse. I just happen to be standing nearby."

She flashed him a smile. "I doubt that excuse would hold up in my father's courtroom."

He didn't much like being reminded of her father. He took a step back. "It's been a long day. I need to get some sleep." And he needed to get to the bunkhouse before Tanner came after him.

"I've been thinking," she said quietly. "You don't look like a criminal to me. You're innocent, aren't you?"

"No, ma'am, I'm not."

And with that, he turned on his heel and headed back to the bunkhouse, his cold words reverberating on the air, echoing through his heart. Until this moment, he'd never experienced the shame of being guilty. Oh, he'd been embarrassed when he'd gotten caught, angry even.

But shame had never slithered through him.

He didn't much like the judge's daughter for making him feel this way.

CHAPTER FOUR

Amelia stood in the kitchen. Three years ago her father had hired Colleen O'Fallon to take care of the house and cook the meals. But Colleen was much more than a servant. She was also the closest thing Amelia had to a best friend, which was the reason Amelia had decided to let Colleen know about her little plan to reform Jesse. He spoke so little that trying to determine what had motivated him to become an outlaw was going to be impossible when she had to sneak around to talk with him. She needed several hours of uninterrupted time.

"I'm thinking that you're playing with fire," Colleen said. Her accent reflected her homeland of Ireland. She was practically a woman of the world, having traveled here by herself on a large ship.

Often Amelia felt like a child when she compared her freedom against that which Colleen's family had granted her. She certainly couldn't see her father letting her travel across a river by herself—much less across an ocean.

Amelia watched Colleen bustle around the kitchen putting away the dishes she'd washed after breakfast.

With her red hair pulled back into a tight bun, Colleen looked older than her twenty-one years.

"But you'll help me, if I manage to pull it off?" Amelia asked.

Colleen came to an abrupt halt and planted her hands on her hips. "Manage to pull it off? When have you not managed to get your way, I want to know?"

"Where the outlaw is concerned. Honestly, Colleen, talking with him is like pulling teeth. It takes a lot of effort but you don't get much for it."

"I didn't think you were supposed to be talking with him at all. If your father finds out about last night—"

"He's not going to find out," Amelia assured her. She knew Jesse wouldn't tell. And she'd deliberately run into Tanner that morning on his way to the cookhouse. He'd promised not to say anything, although he confessed that he'd been watching them with an eagle eye. He'd also warned her not to approach Jesse again.

"I know I was a little bad," she conceded to Colleen. "I wanted to visit with Duchess, and when I saw Jesse standing there I should have come right back to the house, but no harm came out of my talking to him. Except I want to talk with him some more, but I need you to help me with my plan."

"All right, I'll help you, but make a note in that diary you keep that I've got strong reservations about this crazy scheme of yours," she insisted.

With a delighted smile, Amelia threw her arms around Colleen. "Thanks, Colleen. I promise we'll have fun."

"I'm not so sure about that," Colleen said, wiggling out of Amelia's embrace.

"You'll see. Meanwhile, why don't you start to prepare a picnic basket for later in the afternoon?"

She winked at Colleen as she headed out the door. "In case I *manage* to pull off my plan for today, I'll come back and help you finish after I've talked with Papa."

Amelia strolled down the hallway toward her father's library. Each morning before he headed to the county courthouse in Fort Worth, he met with Tanner and her brothers to discuss the day's work schedule. If she was to succeed with her idea, she needed to catch them before her father adjourned the meeting.

Last night she'd been unable to sleep after returning from her midnight excursion to the corral. She simply couldn't get the outlaw out of her mind.

From her father, she knew criminals emphatically stated they were innocent even when they were obviously guilty. What sort of man was Jesse Lawton not to deny his guilt?

She hoped to have a clearer idea by the end of the day. She thought it imperative to understand the criminal mind if she wanted to practice law someday.

She stepped into her father's library. He stood beside his desk with his leather satchel in his hand, which signaled he was ready to wrap up the meeting and be on his way. Her timing was perfect.

"Papa?"

All the men turned and looked at her. She smiled sweetly.

"Papa, Colleen has offered to sew me a new dress for the birthday party you're going to give me. I was wondering if someone could take us into town today to purchase some material and a pattern."

Her father pursed his lips. She knew that habit meant he was contemplating the merits of her request.

"The men have a full schedule," he said.

"But if we don't get started on the dress soon, Colleen might not be able to finish it in time," Amelia said.

Robert shrugged. "I could spare some time today to take Amelia and Colleen into town."

Inwardly Amelia smiled. She'd suspected for some time that Robert might have an interest in Colleen. She'd thought he'd be more willing to take her if she invited Colleen to accompany her.

Her father nodded. "All right then."

Lifting his satchel, he prepared to depart.

"I thought we'd take Jesse with us," Amelia said quickly.

Her father froze in midstride, a surprised look on his face, as though he couldn't quite believe he'd heard her correctly.

"I beg your pardon?" he asked gruffly.

She took a step toward him, clasped her hands in front of her, and tried not to fidget. He had quite an intimidating stare when he set his mind to it—as he had now.

"I noticed he had no bag. And his clothes are atrocious," she explained. "I thought perhaps we should purchase him something a bit tidier."

"He's an outlaw, Amelia," David said.

"I realize that, but I don't understand why we have to make him feel as though he's something to be wiped-off our boots. You wanted to give him a chance to prove himself. It seems to me that improving his self-worth might be in order," she explained.

Robert laughed. "You think new clothes are the answer? Change the shirt and you'll change the man?"

"Not completely. But I know I always feel better when I wear a new dress," she told him, refusing to give up on her idea.

"He's close to Robert's height," Tanner said. "Maybe your brother has some clothes he wouldn't mind giving up."

She stepped closer to her father and met his gaze. "Do you think Jesse has ever owned a new pair of clothes?"

Her father tightened his grip on his satchel before giving a curt nod. "All right. I'll have one of the boys take him to town—"

"That's silly," she interrupted. "To have someone else take him when we're already going. If Jesse causes any trouble, I'm certain Robert can put him in his place." Looking at her brother, she widened her eyes with false innocence. "Couldn't you, Robert?"

"Sure, I could handle him if I needed to," he said with authority.

Men and their pride. She'd learned long ago how to use it to her advantage. Just like last night. She'd known if she told Jesse he could leave if he was scared that he would stay. *Men and their pride,* she thought again.

"She has a point, Judge," Tanner said. "I've got work that needs to be done. Robert going is one thing. Taking a second man away from his duties is another."

Her father reached out and touched her cheek. "You have a good heart, Amelia. I'll approve this trip—but only this trip—because you're right. He could use a little sprucing up. But you're to obey Robert on all matters."

"I will," she promised. "Thank you, Papa."

"I'll see you all this evening." He strode from the room.

Amelia turned to Robert. "I thought we could take the buggy, since we won't be loading up on supplies."

Robert shook his head. "I don't want Colleen sitting in the backseat of the buggy with the outlaw. The wagon might be better. It'll sit three of us on the bench. Jesse can ride in the back."

"Colleen can sit in the front with you. I'll sit beside Jesse," she offered. "The buggy would make for a much more pleasant journey."

Robert narrowed his eyes. "Amelia, why do I feel like I'm being manipulated?"

She smiled brightly and sashayed toward the door, throwing over her shoulder, "Because you are, Robert!"

Jesse focused his attention on the passing countryside—even though it wasn't nearly as pleasant to look at as the young lady sitting beside him.

Amelia was dressed much as she'd been at the train depot. A little hat was perched jauntily on top of her piled-up hair. Her yellow dress matched the wildflowers dotting the landscape.

He could hardly fathom that she was actually sitting beside him, close enough that the slight breeze constantly brought her honeysuckle scent to tease his nostrils.

Robert guided the buggy over the same dirt road they'd traveled yesterday. Colleen O'Fallon sat beside him.

Jesse wouldn't have realized Colleen was a servant if Amelia hadn't told him. No one seemed to treat her as one. They acted like she was more of a friend than someone hired to work for them.

It didn't make sense to him. Just like he couldn't figure out why they were taking him back to Fort Worth to purchase clothes. He didn't much like being beholden to people. He'd have to keep a tally of the expenses today and figure out how many days to add on to his time so he could repay the judge. He didn't want to stay longer than his sentence dictated, but he didn't see any other way to pay the judge back.

"Did you know that Fort Worth is called the Queen City of the Prairie?" Amelia asked.

Jesse turned his attention to her. She sure was pretty. And talkative.

"No, ma'am."

The railroad had arrived in Fort Worth about the time Jesse was heading to prison. He'd noticed yesterday that the town had changed considerably since he'd last seen it.

"I think it's exciting that it's become so important to the cattle industry," she said.

"Amelia, you couldn't care less about the cattle," her brother threw over his shoulder. "You find all the young cattle owners who come to town exciting."

She narrowed her dark green eyes and pursed her lips. "Robert, I don't recall inviting you into this conversation."

"I don't recall hearing a conversation going on. Mostly I just heard you prattling," he said.

Jesse thought he could actually see the fine hairs on the back of her neck bristling.

"I do not prattle," she said sternly. "Besides, if you'd mind your own business, maybe Mr. Lawton and I *could* have a conversation."

Robert chuckled. "I take lessons on minding my own business from you, Amelia."

"Oh, you!" She leaned across the back of the buggy and whapped her brother on the shoulder with her reticule.

Jesse expected Robert to get angry. Instead he simply grinned.

Rolling her eyes, Amelia settled back into her seat. "Brothers can be so irritating," she muttered. She plucked at a thread on her reticule. "Do you have any brothers or sisters, Mr. Lawton?"

"I'd rather you didn't call me that," he said. He wasn't comfortable with the formality or the respect that the title of *mister* indicated.

She peered at him through her lashes. "All right . . . Jesse."

His gut clenched at the way his name rolled off her tongue—like warm honey fresh from a beehive on a hot afternoon.

"You didn't answer my question," she reminded him.

"No brothers or sisters—at least none that I know of," he told her.

"Are you an orphan then?" she asked.

"I've got no family."

She seemed to mull his answer over, and finding it inadequate, asked, "Did you ever know your parents?"

"Nope."

"I'm sorry."

He stared at her. "It's not your fault."

"I didn't mean I thought it was my fault. I was simply expressing my sorrow because I think it's sad—to be an orphan, I mean."

"I got by." He didn't want her sorrow or her pity.

"Not very well if you ended up in prison," Robert said.

Jesse threw the man's back a scathing glare before turning his attention to the passing scenery.

"That wasn't a very nice thing to say, Robert Harper," Colleen said.

"It's the truth. I don't see why I should have to tiptoe around the truth."

"You could be a bit more polite. We're trying to make this a pleasant day for Jesse," Amelia said.

That comment took him by surprise. He snapped his head around to look at her. She was plucking at another thread on her reticule.

No one seemed to know what else to say. Silence wound its way between them. Jesse studied the trees and land that spread out before them. A short while later they joined a throng of buggies, wagons, and horses making their way into Fort Worth.

"Robert, I thought we'd go to Hanson's Dry Goods," Amelia suddenly announced. "It'll save us time, since we'll be able to purchase Jesse's clothes there, and they usually have a nice selection of fabrics."

"I'm all for saving time," Robert said. "And no hat shopping. I don't want to be here until sunset."

Amelia cast a shy glance at Jesse. "He doesn't mean it. If I really wanted to shop for a new hat, he'd let me."

"Don't count on it, Amelia," Robert muttered.

She wrinkled her nose and whispered, "He would."

He figured her brother would let her do just about anything she wanted, since he didn't seem to mind her whapping him on the shoulder.

"I imagine Fort Worth has changed considerably since you were last here," Amelia said quietly.

He almost retorted that he'd been here yesterday, but he figured yesterday didn't count. He'd been too self-conscious about his situation to notice much of anything. Now he seemed to notice it all.

He glanced over at Amelia and nodded. "Yes, ma'am."

"We have two railroads now, and the third should be finished by the end of the year."

Maybe he'd use one of those railroads to leave town once he'd finished serving his sentence.

She smiled brightly. "A few of the businesses— the newspaper office and a couple of the hotels—have telephones."

He stared blankly at her.

"Bein' in prison, he might not know what a telephone is," Colleen offered, accurately interpreting his silence.

Still, did they have to keep bringing up the fact that he'd been in prison—even if she was right? Even if he'd never heard of a telephone?

"I hadn't thought about you not knowing what one is," Amelia said. "It's a machine that allows you to talk to someone you can't even see. Someone who's in another room or another building."

He couldn't begin to imagine how that would work. Or why anyone would want to talk to someone they couldn't see. He wouldn't be able to look into the person's eyes and know what they were thinking. He thought it would make him more uncomfortable than talking to someone he *could* see.

"You might not have noticed it yesterday, but the town has a mule-drawn streetcar that travels a mile of track from the depot to the courthouse," Amelia said.

He shook his head. He hadn't noticed it. He hadn't noticed much of anything except her.

"The car has benches for people to sit on and windows to stop all the dust from the street from getting inside. It makes for a pleasant journey," she told him.

"Unless the car jumps the track," Robert said over his shoulder. "When it does that passengers have to lift it up and put it back on the tracks. I'd rather walk."

"I'm agreeing with Robert," Colleen said. "I'd rather spend my nickel on something else and use my legs to get me where I want to go."

"But the streetcar and the telephone and the gas streetlights are symbols that the town is becoming a city." Amelia looked at Jesse. "Don't you think it's all exciting and important?"

She was looking at him as though she truly wanted to know what he thought.

"I reckon," he said, not wanting to disappoint her.

"Don't you ever say more than two words?"

He shifted in his seat. "I've said more than two words to you."

"But that was miles ago," she told him. "To keep a conversation going you have to add to it. I've been telling you things that you don't know. Tell me something that I don't know. Tell me how Fort Worth is different now than it was when you last saw it."

That was easy enough to do. He held her hopeful gaze and said, "It's bigger."

She laughed, actually laughed, a delightful tinkling sound that reminded him of bells.

"Can you expand on that?" she asked.

"Lot more stores." Clothing stores, leather-goods stores, hotels, banks, coffin builders, bakeries, grocers, lawyers, land agents. All she had to do was look around to see the dealers in lumber, silver, fence wire, and tailored clothing.

"I was hoping for a bit more," she said, still smiling. But he had no more to give her. He looked away from her to the buildings they passed. He didn't want to see Amelia with the twinkle in her eyes and the bright smile.

Pretty Amelia.

Sweet Amelia.

Keep-away-from-her Amelia.

CHAPTER FIVE

Amelia had never understood why men despised shopping.

She'd expected Jesse to be thrilled at the prospect of purchasing new clothes. Instead he scowled and glanced around as though he couldn't wait to get out of the store.

It didn't help matters that Robert seemed equally impatient.

Amelia lifted a chambray shirt off the stack, unfolded it, and held it up. She was slightly disappointed that her attempt to have a conversation hadn't been as successful as she'd hoped. But she didn't plan to easily give up her quest to learn more from him. Thank goodness she'd taken into consideration that it might take him a while to open up more fully. Their time together was only just beginning.

"Turn around, Jesse," she ordered.

"Why?"

She rolled her eyes with impatience at the distrust in his voice. If anyone shouldn't be trusted, it was him.

"So I can get an idea as to whether or not this one will come close to fitting you," she explained.

"It looks right," he said.

"And I'm sure whoever gave you those clothes thought the same thing. Let's be sure, shall we?"

He turned, presenting her with his back, but his stiff stance fairly shouted that he hadn't wanted to comply with her request.

"Uncross your arms," she said.

He did as she ordered, but she could tell he wasn't pleased about having to do it. She found it comforting to know the outlaw reacted the same way that her brothers would if she wanted to measure a shirt against them.

She held the shirt up to his shoulders. Despite the fact that he didn't look as though he'd eaten a decent meal in his entire life, he did have a broad back and wide shoulders.

"Colleen, what do you think?" Amelia asked.

Colleen stopped browsing through the denim britches. "Might work for sitting in church, but I'm thinking he needs more room for working the ranch."

"You're right. We'll go with one a bit larger."

She looked through the stack until she found one that was a little bigger. She took the britches that Colleen handed her and passed them to Jesse. "Hold these against your waist."

Reluctantly he did as she commanded.

"Robert, those should fit him, don't you think?" she asked.

"I reckon."

"Did you even look?" she asked.

"They're britches. Long enough. Wide enough. They'll do for working the ranch," Robert said.

"You're absolutely no help," she told him.

"You didn't say I had to help. You just said I had to bring you to town."

Sometimes her brothers were more trouble than they were worth.

"Fine," she said, ready to move on to the next aspect of her project to tidy Jesse up. "We'll purchase two britches, three work shirts, and a white shirt for special occasions," she said.

"I don't need anything for special occasions," Jesse said.

Ignoring him, she picked out the clothes she would purchase, including a white shirt.

"Colleen and I are going to look at patterns and material now," she told Robert. "I thought you could take Jesse to the barber's."

Jesse still had stubble covering his face, and his hair fell in shaggy waves around his face. She wondered if anyone had bothered to explain to him that the bunkhouse had a bathing room in the back. She wondered if they trusted him with a straight razor. She'd have to talk with Tanner about that.

"Thought you just wanted to get him clothes," Robert said.

"You thought wrong," she said smugly.

Robert sighed. "Do you have any other surprises in store for me?"

"Of course, but if I tell you about them then they won't be a surprise. When we're finished here, we'll meet you at the Peers House," she informed him. She liked the hotel because they had female waiters. She remembered the ruckus that the daring idea had caused.

"All right." Robert turned on his heel. "Jesse, let's go."

She watched Jesse follow her brother out of the store. She could hardly wait to see him spruced up. Surely he wouldn't look as dangerous once his hair was trimmed and his face shaved.

Thank goodness, shopping with Colleen would keep her distracted so she wouldn't get antsy while waiting to see the results of her project.

She turned to Colleen. "Now that we got rid of the men, let's go have some fun shopping."

Colleen laughed. "I'm thinking you've been having fun all morning manipulating every man in your life, starting with your father."

Amelia had to admit that she was enjoying herself. She just wished she knew how to make Jesse open up a little more. The less he talked, the more she wanted him to.

Sitting at a cloth-covered table in the hotel dining area an hour later, Amelia couldn't be happier. She so enjoyed visiting Fort Worth. The city had so much excitement to offer.

She wished she did have time to shop for a new hat, but she had plans for the afternoon, and she didn't want to risk not having enough time to carry them through.

Perhaps she'd marry a city fella. Her father certainly knew enough lawyers and businessmen, and he was inviting them to her birthday celebration. Her brothers knew cattlemen. And they would be coming.

Soon her life could change in ways she'd never dared to imagine.

She took a small sip of hot tea from the china cup before saying to Colleen, "I can't imagine what's taking them so long."

Placing her elbows on the table, Colleen leaned forward. "You know, Jesse didn't look anything like I thought he would. I expected him to look a bit meaner. Perhaps have a scar across his face or rotting teeth or a nose knotted up from all the times it had been broken."

Amelia nodded. "I did, too."

"He certainly doesn't say much," Colleen said.

"I don't imagine one does a lot of socializing in prison. I sorta felt like I was carrying on a one-sided conversation—except when Robert would interrupt with his views on a subject. I really need you to keep him occupied this afternoon so I can talk with Jesse alone."

"I'm not sure Robert will agree to leave you alone with Jesse."

"I don't need to be alone with Jesse. I just need Robert

to be far enough away that Jesse might feel a bit more comfortable talking with me. Besides, I think Robert is sweet on you. I imagine he'll welcome having some time with you."

"Don't be silly." Colleen blushed. "Robert has no interest in the likes of me."

"Of course he does. And you're sweet on him. Admit it. That's the reason you always make his favorite desserts."

"I'll admit I think he's a fine young man."

"Then it shouldn't be a hardship for you to keep him busy this afternoon when I put the next step of my plan into action," Amelia said.

Colleen shook her head. "Why are you so interested in this outlaw?"

"I want to try to figure out why he decided to rob banks." If she could understand that, then the knowledge might help her later if she had to deal with criminals when she became a lawyer.

"He probably started out simple enough. A bit of rebellion. Sneaking around and doing things he shouldn't." Colleen raised a brow. "Like spending time with a young man your father has forbidden you to."

"He forbade me to be *alone* with him," she emphasized. "I've never been completely alone with him."

"I still think you're asking for trouble." Colleen raised her hand and waved. "There's Robert."

Amelia glanced casually over her shoulder . . . and

ceased to breathe as Jesse strode toward her with a confidence he hadn't exhibited before.

The trip to the barbershop had cleaned him up far better than she'd expected it to. His neatly trimmed hair barely touched his collar. Without shaggy black strands falling across his brow, his midnight-blue eyes mesmerized her. With his scraggly beard removed, he didn't appear as rough.

His nose, cheeks, and chin were more prominent—rugged, as though the dry Texas wind had chiseled them from stone with care and precision. Taking its time and striving for perfection.

She couldn't tear her gaze from him. The outlaw was without a doubt one of the handsomest young men she'd ever seen.

CHAPTER SIX

As they traveled back toward the ranch, Jesse tried not to remember the way Amelia had stared at him as he'd walked into the hotel. She'd looked the way he figured he had when he was younger and had slipped beneath the big tent at a circus and watched the trapeze act—mesmerized, unable to believe what he was seeing.

Her eyes had been big and round, her mouth slightly parted.

"Well," she'd finally said. "Don't you look . . . different."

He wasn't certain if looking different was a good thing or not. He'd never gone to a barber before. He'd always cut his own hair using a knife. Looking at his reflection in the mirror of the barbershop, he'd been surprised by his appearance. Although he knew five years had passed, he'd avoided mirrors in prison and had halfway expected to see a fourteen-year-old staring back at him at the barbershop.

It saddened him to see the passing years carved in his face, to see a young man where once there had been a boy. Gazing in the mirror might not have been such a good thing to do.

"Robert, why don't you take that trail up there so we can have a picnic by the river?" Amelia suddenly said, her question more of a statement.

Robert jerked his head around. "You didn't say anything about a picnic."

"I thought I did."

"No, you didn't."

Jesse couldn't get over how much they argued. But there never seemed to be any anger in their words. It was more playfulness than anything. It was obvious they held a great deal of affection for each other. Jesse couldn't imagine arguing with someone and not being angry at the same time. He'd never been around people like these, and they made him uncomfortable. Made him very much aware that he didn't fit in.

"What did you think was in the basket that Colleen put in the back of the buggy?" Amelia asked.

Robert snapped his attention to Colleen. "I reckon I didn't give it much thought. But I didn't have plans for us to take time for a picnic."

"It didn't take us that long in Fort Worth," Amelia said. "Surely we have time for a quick picnic. I'm certain Colleen brought your favorites, didn't you, Colleen?"

Colleen smiled sweetly. "Of course. Fried chicken and buttermilk cake."

Robert shook his head. "I don't know, Amelia. They'll be expecting us . . ."

"Please, Robert. I'd hate to think Colleen went to all that trouble for nothing."

"All right. We'll stop for a little while."

Amelia settled back and shifted her gaze to Jesse. "Do you like picnics?"

He shrugged.

"Don't tell me you've never been on one," she said softly.

"It's eating outside, isn't it?" he asked.

"Yes, it's something like that."

"Well, I've eaten outside."

He wouldn't mind the delay that stopping to eat would grant him. He wasn't in any all-fired hurry to return to the ranch, where everyone watched him as though they expected him to make a mistake, to bolt, or to break one of the judge's rules.

The buggy swayed as Robert guided the horses off the main road onto a less-traveled trail. Amelia bumped against Jesse. Her cheeks burned red as she scooted away from him and held on to her side of the wagon.

It was just a slight touch, but still he felt where her shoulder had brushed against his as though she'd set a hot brand against him. Why was he so aware of everything about her, everything surrounding him? Why did she make him wish he could say he'd been on a thousand picnics, knew all the things she knew, had done all the things she'd done?

Robert brought the buggy to a halt not far from the river. He hopped out, walked swiftly around the horses, and helped Colleen and Amelia climb out of the buggy.

"Jesse, help me unhitch the horses," Robert said, "while the ladies get things ready."

Jesse clambered out of the buggy. He watched as Amelia carried a quilt and Colleen carted a basket to a nearby tree. He turned and found Robert glaring at him.

"Just in case you haven't figured it out yet . . . stay away from Colleen, as well as Amelia, or you'll find yourself back at Huntsville," Robert said.

"Now, remember," Amelia whispered to Colleen, "as soon as we've finished eating, convince Robert to take you for a walk so I can talk with Jesse without Robert's interference."

Colleen glanced over to where Robert and Jesse were leading the horses to the river.

"I'll try, but I don't know if I'll have much luck at it," she said.

Amelia was certain she'd have a great deal of luck. She was sure Robert had a soft spot for Colleen. He'd spent too much time glancing over at her as he'd driven the buggy. It had been funny to watch because every time Colleen looked over at Robert, he'd looked away—

as though he didn't want to get caught.

Sitting on the quilt she'd spread out beneath the boughs of the tree, Amelia removed food from the basket—all the while keeping an eye on Jesse. She'd always heard that the way to a man's heart was through his stomach. She wasn't interested in capturing Jesse's heart, but she did hope that feeding him would put him a little more at ease and cause him to open up a bit more.

She watched as he and Robert began walking toward them—not like friends would, side by side, but as strangers, with Jesse trailing a little behind her brother. Jesse's gaze kept darting toward the river, and she wondered if he was contemplating the merits of escaping.

Escape! Escape! The word thundered through Jesse's mind like a herd of stampeding mustangs.

He was beginning to think everyone was playing a practical joke on him, offering freedom and all the while trying to figure out how to snatch it away.

He was supposed to stay away from Amelia. Stay away from Colleen. And while doing that, he was supposed to sit down and have a meal with them. A picnic.

He felt awkward and ignorant around these people. They didn't seem to measure their words when they spoke to one another. They bickered with no anger. They teased, cajoled, and seemed at ease with one another.

When members of the Nightriders bickered, they

usually came to blows. Jesse had been most comfortable with Sometimes-One-Eyed Pete, but still it was an uneasy partnership, never trusting Pete a hundred percent, never knowing when the gang might abandon Jesse. And abandon him they had.

He knew he had only himself to blame for being sent to prison, but still it rankled.

He followed Robert as they got closer and closer to the tree where Amelia sat on a quilt. Jesse wondered how he was going to manage to eat with these ladies and stay away from them at the same time. Because he definitely did not want to go back to prison.

If someone offered to give him all the money in the world if he'd just return to Huntsville, he'd say no. Nothing on God's green earth was worth going back to prison for. No, sir. He'd do anything, absolutely anything, to stay out of prison. And that included following the judge's rules.

Robert dropped onto an empty space on the quilt.

Amelia patted an area beside her. "Sit here, Jesse."

He hesitated. Was disobeying her going to get him sent back to prison?

"Rather not," he finally managed to say. He glanced at Robert, who nodded. What did that mean? Was it all right to sit beside Amelia, or was he approving Jesse's unwillingness to do so?

Jesse walked past her and sat with his back against

the tree trunk. He was close enough to partake of the victuals, but far enough away that he wasn't really part of the group.

"Jesse, do you like fried chicken?" Amelia asked.

"Yes, ma'am."

He took the chicken leg she handed him and was halfway finished eating it before he noticed Robert wasn't eating the piece he'd been given.

"Most folks wait until everyone is served," Robert said.

Jesse glanced around. Amelia was holding a piece of chicken; Colleen wasn't.

"I'm sure Jesse didn't mean to be rude," Amelia said.

More rules. He'd do better standing by the river until these people were finished with their picnic. He raised his knee, draped his wrist over it, and dangled the chicken over the ground, waiting for everyone to be *served*.

Robert finally took a bite and made a sound deep in his throat that sounded like a gagged cow: "Mmm."

"Colleen knows all Robert's favorite foods," Amelia said. "What's your favorite food, Jesse?"

Anything that filled his belly.

"Don't have a favorite."

"I'm partial to fudge," Amelia admitted. "Colleen, what do you like?"

"I like anything with a bit of sweetness to it," Colleen said.

Jesse started to take a bite of chicken.

"Do you like sweet things, Jesse?" Amelia asked.

He stilled. Sure he liked sweet things. He nodded. "A good-tempered horse."

Robert burst out laughing. Colleen covered her mouth to hide her smile.

Amelia's eyes sparkled. "I meant sweet things to eat."

"Oh." He felt foolish. Outlaws never talked about what kind of food they liked to eat. He didn't fit with these people. Never would. Still, he searched his memory for the last time he'd eaten something sweet and mumbled, "Gumdrops."

Amelia's face lit up. "Lemon?"

He nodded.

"Me, too. If I'd known, I could have purchased some when we were in town."

He shook his head. "I'm already going to have to work extra days at the ranch after I've served my time so I can pay the judge back for everything you purchased for me today," Jesse said. "I don't need gumdrops."

Everyone looked at him as though they were surprised to find him sitting near them.

He looked away from them. He really wished he were standing by the river. Alone. Alone was the way he'd been for most of his life. He was more comfortable with it than sitting with these people and trying to belong.

When they finished eating, Jesse still sat with his back against the tree. Amelia had scooted over a little so she was closer, her profile to him—portrait-perfect pretty.

A short distance away, Robert and Colleen were picking flowers near the river, where the horses had been left to graze. Every now and then Robert darted a quick glance over his shoulder—as though he expected Jesse to be stupid enough to try to escape. Not that the thought hadn't crossed his mind at least a hundred times since he'd stepped off the train yesterday.

He longed for the freedom that running would give him. But the thought of getting caught kept him tethered to the spot. He didn't want to go back to prison.

"I think Colleen likes Robert," Amelia said wistfully. "And he likes her, but they're like two skittish horses prancing around each other."

She looked at him. "Do you think that's the way one goes about courting?"

"How would I know?"

She smiled self-consciously. "I guess there weren't many women in prison."

He glared at her. "None at all."

She blushed becomingly, and Jesse cursed himself for taking his frustrations out on her.

"I'm sorry," he said quietly.

The words sounded strange coming out of his mouth. He couldn't recall ever using them before.

She lifted her gaze to him. "That's all right. I suspect the abrupt change to your life takes a bit of adjustment."

She nibbled on her bottom lip. "Can I ask you a question?"

"You can ask," he told her. "Doesn't mean I'll answer."

She wiggled until she'd inched a bit closer to him. "Why did the leader of the Nightriders gang go by the name of *Sometimes*-One-Eyed Pete?"

"Because he had a glass eye."

Furrowing her brow delicately, she shook her head. "So his name referred to his one good eye?"

"Not exactly. When he played poker and ran out of money, he'd bet his glass eye. If he lost"—he shrugged—"for a while, he'd only have one eye."

She grimaced. "That's rather disgusting."

"Yeah, it could be, but that was Pete."

It had been a long while since he'd spoken so many words strung together. He looked away, feeling strange that he'd said as much as he had. He'd rarely spoken in prison because talking usually led to trouble.

"Why would anyone want someone else's glass eye?" she asked.

"Pete would tell people that a ball of gold was nestled inside the eye. By the time they'd cracked it open and discovered that he'd pulled the wool over their eyes, so to speak, we were halfway to the next town."

"Was the man ever honest about anything?" she asked.

"Some things. He carried out every threat I ever heard him make."

"He sounds like an absolutely charming man," she said.

"He wasn't really."

"I was being sarcastic," she said.

"Oh."

He wasn't much good at talking with a pretty lady. He could discuss the quickest route to take out of town after robbing its bank, could explain the best way to break into a safe, and could describe the particulars of dressing a wound. He didn't think Amelia would be interested in the topics he knew something about.

So he let the silence stretch between them. He listened to the breeze rustling the leaves overhead, the birds twittering, and the occasional neigh of a horse. It was a strange thing, sitting with a girl on a warm afternoon.

He was startled when she reached over and touched the scar on his wrist.

"That must have hurt," she said softly, sympathetically.

He looked at her ivory finger against his tanned skin, and slowly lifted his gaze to her green eyes.

"I'm sorry they hurt you," she said.

He didn't know what to say. No one had ever shown him this much kindness. He felt a knot rise in his throat that made it difficult to swallow. She wasn't supposed to be nice to him. She was supposed to stay away from him.

He glanced toward the river. The last thing he wanted

her brother to see was her touching Jesse's arm. He shifted slightly so her hand fell away from him.

"I've been the one asking all the questions," she said. "Is there anything you'd like to ask me?"

As a matter of fact, he had been wondering about something. He asked, "Do you know if Tanner's ever been to prison?"

He couldn't quite forget the foreman's cryptic comment the night before about understanding that the ranch was far better than prison.

"I've heard he spent some time in a Yankee prison during the war, but he doesn't talk about it," she said.

Jesse hid his disappointment. He'd been hoping that he and the foreman might have something in common. But if Tanner had fought in the war, he was probably close to being a hero. Jesse had never been and never would be a hero.

With an unexpected, delightful smile, Amelia leaned toward him. "I did something terribly wicked today while you and Robert were off at the barber's. If I share it with you, will you promise not to tell a soul?"

Terribly wicked? The judge's daughter?

Well, well, well. So maybe she wasn't the prim and proper lady that he'd suspected her of being.

His mind reeled with the possibilities of what she'd done, and he was more than eager to hear about her notorious behavior.

"I won't tell a soul," he promised.

She smiled brightly, popped to her feet, and raced to the buggy. She came back carrying a package wrapped in brown paper.

"Papa forbids me to have these," she confessed. "But when I saw this one, I just couldn't resist."

She tugged on the string, and Jesse's interest increased. He couldn't imagine what it could be, but whatever it was, she kept it well protected.

Carefully she folded back the paper, and there it was in all its decadent glory: a dime novel. *Lariat Lorena.*

"I've never seen one that featured a woman as the main character," she told him. "I simply had to purchase it, even though Papa doesn't think novels like this one are worth the paper they're printed on."

He couldn't believe it. He absolutely couldn't believe it. *This* was her excursion into wickedness? A book?

He couldn't help himself. He laughed long and hard. Laughed like he'd never laughed in his life.

"What's so funny?" she asked.

"You think *that's*"—he pointed at the book she'd clutched to her chest—"wicked."

"But Papa forbade me to read these books. I thought . . . I thought . . ."

She looked at the book. Then at him. Tears welled in her eyes.

His laughter came to an abrupt end. He hadn't meant

to hurt her feelings. He didn't know how to act around decent folks. Everything he did, everything he said was wrong. Maybe he did belong in prison, away from the world.

He watched with increasing horror as a solitary tear rolled down her cheek. He had no idea what to do around a weeping girl. He didn't even have a handkerchief to give her. "Geez, don't cry."

She sniffed and swiped at a corner of her eye. "You must think I'm terribly stupid."

"Not stupid," he rushed to assure her, trying to think of something he could say to make her feel better. "My reading is just passable. I've never read a book like that one. I'm sure, if you say so, that it's very wicked."

She pouted out her lower lip. "It's not really. That's part of the reason I don't understand why Papa objects to it."

"What's going on over here?" Robert yelled.

Jesse hadn't seen Robert's arrival, but he suddenly found himself jerked to his feet with a fist balled around his shirt and glaring dark eyes boring into him.

Robert shook him. "What did you do to make her cry?"

"Robert!" Amelia jumped up and placed a hand on her brother's arm. "Let him go!"

"What did he do, Amelia?" Robert asked.

"Nothing," Amelia reassured him.

Robert narrowed his eyes into razor-sharp slits. Jesse could see that the man was one wrong word away from throttling him—so he kept his mouth shut. Nothing to be gained by tossing a flame onto a keg of dynamite.

"Robert!" Amelia cried. "He didn't do anything."

"I knew this picnic was a bad idea." Robert shoved Jesse against the tree before releasing him.

"I'm getting the horses and we're heading home." Robert pointed his finger at Jesse. "You don't move from this spot until I have the horses hitched up. Do you understand?"

Jesse nodded. For a brief time, he'd foolishly forgotten that he was still a prisoner. "Yes, sir."

"Robert, you're acting crazy," Amelia protested.

"Amelia, I'm taking care of this matter," Robert ground out, his threatening glare never wavering from Jesse. "You've been manipulating me all morning. And don't think I don't know it. I'm in charge here, and unless you want Father to hear about this incident, you'll do as I say. Now get to the buggy."

Jesse didn't dare look at Amelia, but he heard her indignant huff and the pounding of her footsteps as she trudged away.

"Don't move from this spot," Robert ordered one last time before going after the horses.

Jesse tried to calm his pounding heart, striving to tame his disappointment. All Amelia had needed to do was thrust her stupid book in front of her brother's angry face, so she could explain what had happened.

But doing that would have meant exposing her little *wicked* disobedience.

No one had ever stood up for him before. He'd been a fool to hope that this one time, someone would.

CHAPTER SEVEN

The next morning Amelia saddled her horse Starlight and rode over the vast expanse of land that her family owned. Unlike her brothers, she had no responsibilities that involved the actual running of the ranch. She was responsible for the house—or more precisely, managing Colleen, who needed no managing whatsoever.

Amelia usually took care of any required correspondence, tended to matters that needed her attention, handled any problems that arose, and escaped from the house by late morning. With her father in town presiding over his courtroom or discussing legal matters with the town council, and her brothers working around the Lazy H, her time was pretty much her own. Her father had no problem with her riding over the ranch as long as she didn't wander too far from the main house.

Of course, *too far* was a relative term. What her father considered too far, she often considered not far enough. She found it incredibly inconvenient that he kept such a tight rein on her activities. He would argue that he placed restrictions on her because he loved her and wanted to protect her. A part of her understood his feelings.

But another part of her longed to rebel.

Perhaps that was the reason she'd urged Starlight into a canter and guided the mare along the western portion of the ranch.

Earlier in the morning she'd spotted Tanner in the wagon with Jesse. She figured he planned to put Jesse to work on the fence. Barbed wire was relatively new in this area of the state. Her father wasn't particularly fond of it; cattle tended to get cut up before they realized the twisted tines on the wire could hurt them.

But since her brothers had convinced him that the days of the open range were dwindling, he'd agreed to the investment.

Like her brothers, she usually didn't have much trouble convincing her father of anything. But there were rare exceptions: Jesse being one; Duchess being the other.

Her father was no longer certain the horse was worth keeping. Duchess was proving to be too much for anyone to handle. Amelia hated the thought of losing her. The mare was usually gentle unless someone attempted to ride her. Then she went a little crazy—a mild word for the horse's reaction, considering one cowboy had broken his arm and another had busted his leg while trying to tame the beast.

Amelia released a sigh. If only the horse weren't so beautiful with her black, shiny coat that looked almost blue. If only Amelia didn't already care about the animal so much.

She lifted a hand to shield her eyes from the harsh afternoon sun. In the distance she saw a man working on the fence, wire coiled around his feet. It was Jesse, and he was alone, the wagon nowhere in sight. Usually two or three men worked on the fencing, but she imagined no one wanted to work beside the outlaw.

Still, she was surprised Tanner had left him alone. Although Jesse couldn't cover any great distance quickly by walking—which made an escape attempt impossible—she thought it seemed a little unkind to expect him to labor with no companionship.

As though he was . . . well, what he was. An outlaw.

Although she sensed that even if he were surrounded by a dozen cowboys, he'd still look lonesome. He'd seemed so uncomfortable yesterday during the picnic. She'd hoped by sharing her book with him that she'd be able to get him to relax. Instead she'd managed to get him into trouble.

She thought about heading back to the house. Jesse intrigued her, but she'd expected to find others here. Talking to him by the corral knowing that Tanner was watching was one thing. Spending the day with him while Robert kept vigil was also acceptable. But approaching Jesse here, where she would be completely alone, might be foolhardy.

Although she truly didn't believe he'd harm her. Of

course, there had always been someone near enough to keep him tethered.

Quickly she looked around to make certain he was alone. No one was in sight. She'd have to talk with him another time. She lifted the reins to turn her horse at the same time that Jesse glanced back over his shoulder.

Even with his hat shadowing his face, she sensed his intense gaze settling on her. Too late. She couldn't leave now without appearing to be afraid of him, and she certainly wasn't afraid of him.

At least, not terribly frightened. Still, she couldn't forget that he'd admitted he was guilty. Jesse Lawton was about as bad as they came. He wasn't a stray puppy to be taken in and cuddled. He was an outlaw serving out his time under her father's strict rules.

He went back to work, pulling the wire tight before hammering it into place against the post with a nail. Simply dismissing her as though she were nothing more than a bee buzzing around.

She couldn't leave now, not after he'd seen her. She didn't want him to think he had any power over her at all. But as she nudged her horse forward, her stomach quivered as though she'd swallowed a field of butterflies.

She brought Starlight to a halt a short distance away from Jesse. With each of his movements, his shirt stretched taut across his back. When he twisted slightly, she saw that he'd loosened several buttons, giving the gentle breeze the opportunity to cool his skin. He'd rolled up his sleeves, revealing the corded muscles on his forearms and the scars on his wrists.

"I was looking for Tanner," she lied, not willing to admit she'd actually been hoping to find Jesse.

He stopped hammering, tipped his hat off his brow with his thumb, and challenged her with his gaze. "He's not here."

"Well, I can see that. Do you happen to know where he is?"

He shrugged. "I reckon he figured I didn't need to know his business."

"I'm surprised he left you alone."

She thought he could cut through the barbed wire with the narrowed gaze he shot at her.

"Surprised he trusted me not to run off?" he asked.

She shifted over the saddle. "No." Although that had been the first thought that had flashed through her mind.

"I'm surprised he left you alone to do a job that usually two or three men handle. Isn't it difficult to hold the wire and hammer it into place at the same time?"

She knew that typically one man stretched it while another nailed it to the post. Two men usually dug and planted the posts.

He shrugged. "I'm handling it."

"But it doesn't seem fair—"

"Life's not fair," he interrupted.

She completely understood that sentiment. If life were fair, her mother wouldn't have died. Still the outlaw baffled her. "Why are you working so hard?"

He blinked, and she could see his dark eyebrows drawing together as though her question confused him.

"Tanner said he needed the fence put up."

"You could take a nap, and he'd never know. You could simply sit against a post—"

"The day would go too slow. I've got over eighteen hundred days to serve. The more quickly they go, the sooner I can get on with things."

Almost two thousand days of being watched, of being told what to do and when to do it. Perhaps her life wasn't the prison she'd always thought it was.

"What will you do when you've finished your time?" she asked.

"That's my business."

He reached out and snagged his canteen off a nearby post. She watched with fascination as he tipped his head back and slowly drank. Sweat beaded his throat, and his Adam's apple slid up and down with each swallow.

He brought the canteen away from his mouth. His lips were damp. He really had very nice lips. She remembered the way they'd looked in laughter. But she hadn't seen him simply smile with enjoyment.

"Do you ever smile?" she asked.

He presented her with his back. "Look, I've got work to do."

"You can be sociable for a little while," she said, more tartly than she'd intended. She didn't much enjoy being ignored.

He spun around so quickly that she jerked back on the reins. The horse whinnied and sidestepped.

"Don't you understand that if the judge finds out that I've been talking with you, he'll send me back to prison?"

"I'd explain that it wasn't your fault."

He glared at her. "Like you explained yesterday?"

Her stomach quivered at the reminder that she might not have stood up to her brother as she should have.

"I told Robert nothing happened," she snapped in her own defense.

"Maybe you didn't notice, but he wanted nothing more than to pound his fist into my face."

"But he didn't do it, did he? Because I convinced him not to," she told him.

"You didn't convince him of anything. You were too worried he'd find out about your *wicked* little book," he retorted angrily.

"It's not a wicked book," she said tartly. "Father simply prefers for me to read something else."

Snorting, he shook his head and went back to work. "And I prefer for you to be somewhere else," he muttered.

Strangely, at this moment she wanted to be right where

she was. Especially since he was actually giving her more than two words at a time. She'd prefer they weren't laced with anger, but at the moment she was willing to take whatever she could get.

"If I'd truly thought Robert was going to hit you, I would have explained exactly what had happened," she assured him.

"Sure you would have."

"I would have." She wanted to stomp her foot, but that was a little hard to do when it was resting in a stirrup.

She almost felt as though she were arguing with one of her brothers. But her feelings toward Jesse didn't run along the lines of sibling rivalry.

He intrigued her because of the things he'd experienced that she never would. He'd apparently been on his own at an early age, experienced freedom she could only imagine. That he'd chosen to squander his opportunities amazed her. Perhaps his reticence was partly to blame. His social skills were sorely lacking. She decided that if she had to, she'd force him to be sociable.

"What's it like living in prison?" she asked.

He stilled, the thick gloves he wore to protect his hands curling around the wire. "You don't want to know."

"Yes, I do."

"Why?" He glared at her over his shoulder.

"I'm simply trying to be friendly."

"Lady, you don't want to be friends with me, and I

don't want to be friends with you. All I want is to serve my days in peace."

"If you keep snapping every time someone asks you a question, you'll serve your days alone."

"Which is fine by me."

He straightened out the wire, tugged on it, and proceeded to nail it into place on the next fence post. The more he ignored her, the more she didn't want to be ignored.

She couldn't fathom why she was fascinated with him. A couple of the cowboys who worked the ranch were nicer. None had ever been to prison. They all enjoyed her company.

So why was this one so cantankerous? She'd figured he'd welcome a little conversation.

"You don't mean that," she stated emphatically.

"Why wouldn't I mean it?" he asked.

"Why would you *choose* to be alone?"

"So I wouldn't have to listen to you harping at me all the time."

Indignation caused her to sit straighter in the saddle. "I do not harp."

"You do, too."

"I do not."

"You're harping right now."

She tightened her hold on the reins. Was she harping at him?

"I'm trying to engage you in a conversation," she told him.

"I'm not interested."

"How can you not be interested?"

"Because being interested can get me sent back to prison," he ground out.

"So it's not that you don't like me; it's that you don't like prison."

"I'll do whatever it takes to stay out of prison. And if that means ignoring you, then I'll ignore you."

Well, she supposed she couldn't fault him for that attitude. Still, there was no one to see, so where was the harm in having a little conversation? If he learned to be a bit more sociable, everyone might accept him more, and she wouldn't have to sneak around in order to speak with him.

She waited patiently while he stretched the wire over to the next post and nailed it into place. Then she blurted out what had been troubling her all morning. "My father's decided that if Duchess isn't broken by the end of the week, he's going to get rid of her."

The outlaw stilled and turned to her slowly, as though he knew it wouldn't take much to make her burst into tears.

"What do you mean, get rid of her?" he asked.

It seemed she'd finally found a subject that interested him. Shrugging, she fought back the tears stinging her eyes. "I don't think he'll put her down, but he's concerned that the horse is mean. And if she is, then she's no good for riding, no good for breeding."

"Wouldn't you feel mean if you were kept in a small

enclosure all day?" he asked.

"If someone could break her, I'd take her galloping across the ranch. We have two thousand acres. That ought to be enough freedom for her. I love her. I can't stand the thought of losing her," she explained.

"Maybe he'll just put her out to pasture," he offered.

She shook her head. "He'll probably sell her off or take her back to her original owner. My father believes everything should have a purpose."

"So why are you telling me all this?"

Why, indeed?

"I don't know. I suppose because you were visiting with Duchess the other night."

"I wasn't visiting with her," he retorted. "I just walked to the corral and she was there."

"Well, pardon me all to heck. I thought maybe you might care, but I forgot that you're an outlaw and don't care about anything or anyone other than yourself."

Frustrated with the outlaw, Amelia kicked Starlight's flanks and sent the mare galloping toward home. She didn't know why she bothered to give the time of day to Jesse Lawton.

He was the most unsociable creature she'd ever met, and her attempts to be his friend only frustrated her. She didn't know why she'd blurted out her worries about Duchess. She'd been looking for a sympathetic ear, and Jesse didn't have a sympathetic bone in his body.

So much for her worry that she'd feel bad sending a man to prison. She could send an outlaw like Jesse to prison with pleasure.

He obviously didn't care about her troubles. For the next eighteen hundred days or so, she'd be certain to avoid him.

CHAPTER EIGHT

Amelia Harper had the prettiest smile Jesse had ever seen. And until this moment, he hadn't realized she'd never bestowed one quite like it on him.

But she was sure flashing it at the cowboys who had gathered around her at the corral. It seemed he wasn't the only one she'd told about her father threatening to get rid of the mare.

Every cowboy with a pair of spurs was determined to break that horse for her.

Jesse stood off to the side near the corral while the cowboys gathered around the judge's daughter the way bees were attracted to the brightest flower in the field. He thought about going to the bunkhouse, but he enjoyed watching her when she was happy—as she seemed to be right now.

Although he didn't particularly like seeing how Mitch Monroe was looking at her. The ranch hand wore a wide grin that said he thought he was something special, and that Mitch figured Amelia thought the same thing. Of course, the way she was gazing up at Mitch, maybe she did think he was amazing.

Jesse didn't want to contemplate the reasons that notion bothered him. He knew Amelia would never favor him. His past would always serve as a wall between them, and that was just fine with him. Or at least, he told himself it was.

Still, he couldn't quite forget she was the one who had been responsible for getting him some new clothes. He hated to admit how much he enjoyed wearing them. He didn't feel quite so out of place. And the men weren't looking at him with as much challenge in their gazes as they had that first night.

"What kind of reward are you gonna give the fella who breaks that ornery mare for you?" Mitch asked.

Amelia glanced around before announcing, "Well, I was thinking something special. Since you're all invited to my birthday dance, the fella who breaks Duchess gets the first dance."

Mitch moaned. "Ah, Amelia, that's not special. Reckon every fella here will get a dance by night's end. You're asking us to risk our bones for something every fella might get. It needs to be something precious." He grinned broadly. "How 'bout a kiss?"

Before she could answer, the cowboys were whooping. Even from this distance, Jesse could see her cheeks turning pink.

"Mitch Monroe, that's an awfully bold request," Amelia chastised.

Mitch widened his grin. "I'm a bold cowboy, darlin'. A kiss from you is worth risking a bone or two."

Jesse wondered where the judge and her brothers were, wondered how they'd feel about Mitch's suggestion.

Amelia glanced around. Jesse thought she looked a bit uncertain. Then she thrust up that delicate chin of hers.

"All right. A kiss it is."

More whistles and whooping from the men followed her pronouncement.

"I'm gonna break that horse for you, Amelia," Mitch said.

Her smile blossomed. "Be careful, Mitch."

"Don't you worry none. Just have that thank-you kiss waiting for me when I get back."

Jesse didn't want to ponder what her kiss might taste like or acknowledge the spear of envy that shot through him when he thought about her kissing someone else. *Someone else?* When had he started thinking about her kissing him?

Mitch sauntered into the corral with a confidence that Jesse found irritating. From the moment Tanner had introduced Mitch to him earlier in the day, Jesse had felt disgust toward him emanating from Mitch.

Tanner had saddled the horse and was holding it at the ready in the center of the corral. He'd covered the mare's eyes with a large bandanna to keep it calm. It seemed everyone wanted to make sure Amelia kept the mare.

Amelia moved up to the fence, and the remaining cowhands followed, all crossing their arms over the top railing.

Jesse was off to the side, not part of the group. Frank Garrison moved up to stand at Amelia's right. He seemed like a decent enough fella. At least he wasn't making promises about breaking the horse that he couldn't keep. Wasn't prodding Amelia to give him a kiss.

Jesse shifted his gaze to the corral. Tanner was holding Duchess while Mitch mounted her. Mitch gave a brisk nod, and Tanner ripped away the bandanna. He scurried toward the corral and scrambled over the fence near the spot where Jesse stood.

Duchess wasted no time in bucking off her rider. Mitch landed with a thud that stirred up the dust around him. The horse kicked the air another time or two before trotting over to a distant corner.

Everyone seemed as disappointed as Amelia that Mitch hadn't met with more success.

"I'll give it a try," Frank announced, but his voice didn't carry much confidence.

Jesse figured the cowboy would be lucky to come away with everything intact. A horse could sense a rider's mood.

Mitch got up and started hitting the dust off his britches. "No, I'll try again."

Standing beside Jesse, Tanner mumbled, "I know Mitch is sweet on Amelia and wanting that kiss, but I swear that horse is more stubborn than most of the women I know."

"That's because he's trying to break her," Jesse said quietly.

"How else are you going to ride her?" Tanner asked.

"You tame her."

Tanner propped his elbow on the fence and stared at Jesse. "You say that like you know how to do it."

Jesse shrugged. "Maybe I do."

Mitch had started twirling a lasso within the confines of the corral, slowly walking toward Duchess.

"That's just gonna spook her," Jesse told the foreman.

"Mitch, hold off!" Tanner yelled.

The cowhand turned around, the rope going limp in his hand. "I gotta catch her so I can ride her again."

"I'm gonna give Jesse a chance to tame her," Tanner suddenly announced.

Jesse couldn't have been more surprised if Tanner had proclaimed Jesse to be a free man.

Mitch barked out his laughter. "What's an outlaw know about breaking a horse?"

"Reckon we'll find out," Tanner said. He nudged Jesse's shoulder. "Go on. Show us what you know."

Jesse felt as though he'd gotten railroaded into doing this. He hadn't volunteered to do it. He'd only mentioned that he might know how. Saying no was on the tip of his tongue, but he made the mistake of sliding his gaze over to Amelia.

She was looking at him as though he had the makings of a hero. Backing out was no longer an option—not because he considered himself a hero, but simply because he couldn't bring himself to disappoint Amelia. He didn't take the time to reflect on the reasons he was feeling as he was.

He simply bent his body and slipped between two slats of the fence.

Glaring at him through narrowed eyes, Mitch held the rope out to him.

Jesse sauntered past him. "Won't need it."

"You're gonna land on your backside, boy," Mitch called after him.

Jesse didn't think so, because he knew something Mitch didn't. He knew the horse. And the horse knew him.

For the past two nights, with Tanner's permission, Jesse had returned to the corral and bedded down beneath the vast expanse of black sky and twinkling stars . . . and Duchess had kept him company.

"What's going on?"

Amelia nearly jumped over the railing at the unexpected boom of her father's voice. He wedged himself between her and Frank. Her brothers took up their posts on the other side of her.

They'd all been in her father's library going over the ledgers. She'd hoped they'd stay there until Duchess was broken. She didn't want her father to see any more injured cowboys.

More than that, she didn't want her father to see her give Jesse his reward if he did manage to break Duchess. Had Jesse heard her promise to give a kiss to anyone who broke the horse? She never would have agreed to Mitch's suggestion that a kiss should be the prize if she'd truly believed someone could tame Duchess. But after all these weeks, with no one having any luck, she'd felt safe in offering a kiss, because she didn't think anyone would collect it.

She'd simply been engaging in a little harmless flirtation with Mitch. She certainly hadn't expected Jesse to take part in the contest.

"Jesse's going to try to break Duchess," she said, surprised to find she sounded out of breath with anticipation. Not only might her horse get broken, but she'd have the opportunity to openly watch Jesse without having to slide sly glances his way.

With all the men surrounding her, she'd still been acutely aware of Jesse's presence a short distance away. She knew Mitch was sweet on her. Mitch was more reputable than Jesse. Mitch warranted her undivided attention. Yet Jesse intrigued her.

"Amelia, it's time to admit that purchasing this horse was a mistake," her father said quietly.

"I love her."

Her father sighed. "It's a horse, not a person."

She glanced up at him, her heart in her eyes. "Please, don't send her away."

"We'll see." He looked back toward the corral, and Amelia did the same.

Her heart began to pound at the sight of Jesse standing beside Duchess—simply standing beside her and rubbing her neck as though he had all day to do so, as though the sun hadn't already begun to set and invited in twilight.

She thought she detected Jesse's lips moving. Was he talking to Duchess?

She had a penchant for talking to animals, but she'd never expected that anyone else did other than an occasional "giddyap!"

But Jesse seemed to be sharing secrets with Duchess, and Amelia was surprised to discover she was envious of the attention he was giving the horse. He certainly never seemed interested in talking with her!

As Mitch hoisted himself over the fence, men moved out of his way so he could stand beside her father.

"Likely to get himself killed," Mitch said, "but I don't reckon that'll be any great loss."

"Losing a life is always something to be mourned," her father said.

"Didn't mean no disrespect, Judge; just figured with him bein' an outlaw and all . . ." Mitch's voice trailed off, no doubt because her father didn't seem to be listening.

He was concentrating on Jesse. Amelia wondered if he

was worried about Jesse leaping on the horse's back and escaping to freedom.

Jesse gripped the saddle horn with one hand.

Amelia held her breath.

Without using the stirrup, he managed to throw himself onto the saddle in a fluid movement that Amelia had barely a second to appreciate before Duchess began bucking wildly.

But unlike Mitch, who had lost his balance and his hold with the first kick of the mare's hind legs, Jesse hung on. Although Amelia wasn't certain that *hanging on* was the way to describe the manner in which he rode the horse.

He didn't hold his body stiffly as Mitch had. Instead, he seemed to flow with Duchess, almost as though they were one. With one hand clutching the saddle horn, he raised the other for balance.

Duchess began to kick less, to take several quick steps before bucking again.

A few more steps. A twist. A kick. A gallop. A trot.

And then she was cantering around the corral as though it were the most natural thing in the world for her to do.

At that moment, Amelia thought she could have heard a leaf land on the ground as an unnatural hush descended around them. No one had expected the horse to settle into an easy lope. No one had expected Amelia to have to keep her word and give a kiss to the outlaw.

Jesse brought the horse to a halt, swung one long leg back, and dismounted. Holding on to the reins, he started walking toward her. Her heart slammed against her ribs each time his foot landed on the ground, bringing him closer to her.

Step. *Thump-thump.* Step. *Thump-thump.* Step. *Thump-thump.*

His battered hat shaded his eyes, and she couldn't determine what he might be thinking.

She was trying to figure out if she should warn her father that she was going to kiss the outlaw, or if she should just quickly give him his reward and hope for the best.

Jesse stopped a few feet away from her.

"You probably ought to let one of the hands ride her for a day or two, just to make sure she doesn't get skittish about carrying another rider," he said quietly.

She nodded, her voice trapped somewhere behind the knot that had risen in her throat.

"I've never seen anyone talk to a horse before," Robert said. "What did you say to her?"

"Nothing of importance. Just something to calm her."

"Where did you learn to break a horse like that?" David asked.

"Prison." The solitary word sliced through the air as though it were a rapier, serving as a reminder that he was very different from all the other cowhands gathered around her.

Unlike them, he never had a ready smile. She'd heard him laugh only once. He'd built an invisible wall to separate them, a wall she wasn't certain she wanted to clamber over or knock down.

"I recall the warden telling me you took good care of the horses," her father said.

"Yes, sir." He jerked his thumb over his shoulder. "I'll go ahead and unsaddle this one and brush her down, if that's all right."

"That'll be just fine. Last stall on your right in the barn," Robert said.

She didn't think Jesse's gaze had wavered from her during his entire conversation with her father and brothers. He hesitated before turning on his heel and heading toward the barn, acknowledging with his leaving that the prize she'd offered to the others was forbidden to him.

"Jesse, wait!" Amelia called out.

She scrambled through the slats and walked quickly toward where Jesse was waiting.

"Amelia!" her father called after her.

She knew she should answer her father, but she didn't know how much longer her courage was going to stay with her.

"Your reward," she said breathlessly.

"Don't do it." His lips barely moved, and his voice was incredibly low.

But she did. She rose up on the tips of her toes and

quickly bussed a kiss across his cheek.

She watched him swallow hard just before he ducked his head and strode toward the barn.

He'd risked breaking his bones, getting hurt in order to tame Duchess for her . . . and all she'd been willing to risk was a quick peck on his cheek.

Tears stung her eyes because she'd seen the truth in his—if he'd been anyone else, she would have kissed him properly.

But he was an outlaw.

CHAPTER NINE

"What in thunderation did you think you were doing in that corral?"

Standing within her father's library, Amelia tipped up her chin and met his gaze squarely. "Keeping my promise."

With his hands gripping the desk as though that action were the only thing that kept him from launching himself over the top, he narrowed his eyes. "And what promise would that be?"

"I promised to kiss whoever broke the horse for me. I didn't really think anyone would have the gumption to try—anyone other than Mitch. Otherwise I wouldn't have offered a kiss as a prize. I certainly didn't expect Jesse to accomplish what no one else had been able to. But once he had, I couldn't very well go back on my word."

She felt her brothers scrutinizing her. They stood just off to the side, arms crossed. They weren't any happier with her than her father was.

With a sigh, he dropped into his chair. "I told you to stay away from him. I know I allowed him to go with you on the trip to town, but I thought you understood it was an exception to the rule and was not to be repeated. Nor did it cancel out the rules I laid down."

"Tanner was at the corral, and almost every ranch hand. I couldn't have been any safer than I was. Besides, if he were truly dangerous, Papa, would you have brought him here?"

"That's not the point, Amelia," Robert scolded. "Father gave you an order—"

"I'm seventeen years old," she interrupted.

"Not yet, you're not," David said.

"Soon enough," she reminded him. "For pity's sake, it was a kiss on the cheek. I doubt anyone thinks anything of it."

She was trying not to think about it herself, but she couldn't quite erase from her mind his plea for her not to kiss him. His request had run deep. For a second she'd thought she'd sensed fear in his voice.

He'd no doubt been afraid that her father would send him back to prison if she kept her promise. Standing here now, she could only hope that he didn't.

"I want you to stay away from him," her father said.

"Did you notice how different he looked today?" she asked. "With his hair cut shorter and his new clothes?"

Her father nodded. "I noticed. I hardly recognized him when I first saw him."

"Imagine how much he might change if we stopped treating him like an outlaw."

"A tiger can't change its stripes," David said.

Amelia wanted to shriek. "David, I'm talking to Papa."

"I'm just offering my thoughts on the matter."

"Papa—"

He held up his hand. "Jesse has only been here two days. Let's take it slow. See how it goes. You were right about him needing some new clothes. You've done your good deed. Now obey my rules."

Sometimes it was simpler to just give in. "Fine. I'm going to see if supper is ready."

She pivoted on her heel and strode from the room, working hard to hold her anger in check. She marched down the hallway and shoved open the door to the kitchen.

"When will supper be ready?" she demanded.

Colleen turned from the oven and planted her hands on her narrow hips. "When it's good and cooked, lass. Who put a bee in your bonnet?"

Amelia slumped into a nearby chair and crossed her arms. "Papa treats me as though I'm a child."

"Because you're *his* child," Colleen said, relaxing her challenging stance.

"But it's not fair!"

"Little in life is. Your da is a good man, doing the best he can with what he's got."

"But Colleen, you're only four years older than me. You left your family and crossed an ocean for a new life. I get a tongue-lashing for crossing the corral."

Although that wasn't exactly true. She'd gotten into

trouble for approaching Jesse—and more, for giving him a kiss.

"I think there's more to it than that," Colleen said as she moved to the stove. "Why would you be crossing the corral?"

Colleen pinned Amelia to the spot with her stare.

"I had to give Jesse . . . something."

Colleen began stirring the thick soup in the pot. Robert was partial to soup.

"So it's that outlaw who'd be causing the trouble then?" Colleen asked.

"Not exactly." Amelia sat up a little straighter. "I don't know why everyone acts as though he's so dangerous. All he did was rob a bank."

Colleen laughed. "Well, now, aren't you sounding like you've lost your good sense? You wouldn't think it was such a little thing if it was your hard-earned money he took."

"I know it's not a little thing." Her frustration with the situation growing, Amelia got up and crossed the kitchen so she was standing beside Colleen. "He just looks as if he doesn't expect much from the world. Looking at him, I could tell he didn't think I'd keep my promise and kiss him, and knowing he felt that way made me want to. And so I did."

Colleen's blue eyes widened. "You kissed him, lass? No wonder your da is upset."

"It was just a peck on the cheek."

Colleen waved her hand in the air. "Well, then, it doesn't hardly count, does it?"

"Doesn't count at all," Amelia assured her. Although even as she said it, a part of her knew she was lying.

For some reason she was left with the distinct impression that it did count. It counted a great deal.

Five hours later, stretched out on his bed, his hands behind his head, his gaze on the ceiling, Jesse could still feel the brush of Amelia's lips across his cheek. Her touch had been soft, like a butterfly landing lightly upon a petal.

He'd breathed in her sweet honeysuckle scent, carried it deeply into his lungs, as though holding on to it could erase all else. A crazy notion.

He'd been holding his breath because he'd expected at any moment for Judge Harper to order that he be returned to prison. He'd told her not to do it for so many reasons that he could barely sort them out in his mind.

He was afraid she'd get in trouble, worried that he'd be sent back to prison, terrified that one touch wouldn't be enough. He'd gone so long without kindness that he'd decided the only way he could survive was to avoid it completely.

As long as he didn't actually experience what he'd been missing, he could pretend that his chest didn't ache with the wanting of it.

In the darkness he heard a bed creak, followed by

footsteps so quiet that he had to strain his ears to hear them. They were coming closer. He tensed, prepared to fight if need be.

The bed below him moaned as though someone had stepped on it, and then suddenly he was face-to-face with a darkened silhouette as someone hovered over him.

"Stay away from Amelia," the shadow whispered harshly. "She belongs to me."

He recognized the voice. Mitch Monroe.

"Does she know that?" Jesse asked calmly. After spending five years with men who'd just as soon kill him as look at him, he wasn't threatened by the cowhand—even if he was a little bigger than Jesse.

"All that matters is that you know that."

The shadow retreated, and Jesse slowly uncoiled his body. His heart was pounding so hard he could actually hear it.

He wasn't looking for trouble, but it had obviously found him. It always did.

Most of the cowhands ate their breakfast inside the cookhouse, sitting at one of several long, planked tables.

But Jesse took advantage of having the freedom to eat anywhere he wanted. He took his tin plate with its eggs, biscuits, and gravy outside. He sat beneath the windmill, with his back against the barrel at its base, listening to the steady clacking as the wind did its job. The barrel held the water that was pumped into the nearby buildings.

He had to admit that the ranch cooking was considerably better than prison fare. As a matter of fact, everything about the ranch was better than prison. He washed up with warm water instead of cold. He had soap so he could lather his face when he shaved. If he couldn't sleep, he could walk outside.

Which he'd done again last night after Mitch had spoken to him. He tried not to think about Amelia giving her attention to Mitch. He tried not to think about Amelia at all.

He glanced up as Frank Garrison walked toward him. The young cowhand's legs curved out so it appeared as though he still sat on his horse. With his plate in his hand, Frank crouched before Jesse, balancing himself on the balls of his feet.

"I bet Mitch two bits that you wouldn't tell Tanner we left you alone at the fence yesterday," he said.

Jesse simply met his gaze. Frank and Mitch had been given the task of helping him with the fence. Instead they'd decided to go swimming in a nearby river.

"So now I'm two bits richer." Frank grinned. "So how come you didn't report us to Tanner?"

"He didn't ask."

Frank started shoveling his eggs into his mouth. His earnest face looked as though he'd never known a day of hardship.

"Well, I figure one good turn deserves another. I overheard your visitor last night." He didn't stop eating even though he was talking. "Reckon you ought to know how things stand around here. Judge Harper has forbidden anyone to court Amelia until she turns seventeen, and Mitch has kinda let it be known that he intends to court her proper as soon as she's old enough."

"So why tell me?"

Frank stopped chewing and blinked. "Well, so you don't get on his bad side. I mean, don't get me wrong, Mitch is my friend and all, but he's got a bit of a temper."

"I'll keep that in mind."

"That's good, 'cuz we all know if you do one thing wrong, the judge is sending you back to prison," he said around the biscuit in his mouth.

"Why do you care?"

Frank looked surprised. "I don't. Well, not really . . . I mean . . ." He swallowed before meeting Jesse's gaze. "Heck fire! We've been trying to break that mare for more than six weeks. How did you do it?"

Jesse shrugged. "I wasn't trying to break her; I was just trying to gentle her."

No need to reveal that he'd whispered to the horse that she'd be mighty fortunate to have Amelia riding her. Or that the horse recognized his scent and trusted him. That the horse hadn't been terrified of him, just wary.

Frank nodded. "Well, you gentled her, all right. I

already took her out for a ride this morning. She's a fine animal when she's not bucking. Anyway, since I respect what you did yesterday—both with the horse and not telling on us—I just wanted to explain why Mitch paid you a midnight visit. So there's no misunderstanding in the future."

"Frank!"

Frank jerked back and landed on his backside. Jesse lifted his gaze to see Mitch storming toward them.

"What are you doing talking to the criminal?" Mitch demanded.

Frank picked up his plate and stood. "Nothing."

Mitch glared at Jesse. "You're asking for trouble."

Frank released an uncomfortable laugh. "No, he's not. Come on, we need to report to Tanner."

Mitch pointed his finger at Jesse. "I'm not afraid of you."

"You should be," Jesse said evenly, adding a gravelly pitch to his voice. It was his prison voice. The way he'd talked in prison—with no emotion. It was the only way to survive. To make it sound as though he cared about nothing. A man who cared about nothing had nothing to lose, and that attitude made him all the more dangerous.

"Come on," Frank said, tugging on Mitch's arm. "We need to get to work."

"You keep asking for trouble and you're gonna find it," Mitch warned before he turned to go.

Jesse could have argued that he hadn't asked for it. Frank had approached him. He would have been content to eat his meal alone.

Instead he kept his mouth closed and simply watched them walk away.

CHAPTER TEN

Amelia brought Duchess to a halt near the corral. David had insisted on riding with her in case the horse decided to rebel.

But she'd been remarkably docile. Oh, a time or two, she'd tried to break free, but a gentle tug on the reins had brought her back under control. With each passing moment, Amelia's love for the horse grew.

"Guess you're gonna brush her down now," David said.

She smiled at him. "Yep. Thanks for riding with me."

"My pleasure."

"You're only saying that because it gave you an excuse not to check on the herd first thing this morning."

He looked wounded. "Ah, Amelia. How could you think such a thing?"

"Because I know you," she said with a laugh.

"Reckon you do at that. I'd better get to work." He turned his horse about. "Hey, listen, will you ask Colleen to bake me a blackberry cobbler for dessert?"

"Sure." Since blackberry cobbler was also a favorite of Robert's, she figured Colleen would comply with the request.

David tipped his hat at her before urging his horse into a full gallop. When her brothers weren't being unreasonably protective, she enjoyed their company.

She dismounted, grabbed the reins, and led Duchess into the barn. Dust motes danced through the sunlight filtering through the wide-open doors and the open windows in the loft. She was both surprised and pleased to see Jesse mucking out one of the stalls. It was a task that no one welcomed, but that someone had to do. Tanner rotated the chore among the men.

She came to a halt outside the stall where Jesse was working. He had to have been aware of her presence, but he ignored her. She wondered if he'd thought about the kiss she'd given him yesterday evening. She'd drifted off to sleep thinking about it.

"Morning," she said softly.

He stilled, and she saw his fingers tighten around the broom handle. He slowly looked over his shoulder. "Morning."

With a hesitant smile, she pointed at the horse behind her. "I took Duchess for a ride this morning."

He straightened and faced her. "How'd she do?"

She broadened her smile. "She did wonderfully."

"Glad to hear it."

She took a step closer. "I was impressed with the way that you gentled her. You made it look so easy."

"Nothing easy about it. Just a matter of not making her more frightened than she already was."

"Have you ever captured a wild horse?" she asked.

"Sure. A fella doesn't have much choice if he needs one and can't afford to buy one."

"Are you as skilled at capturing a horse as you are at breaking one?"

He furrowed his brow. "I had a fair amount of luck at it from time to time, years back."

Her excitement mounted as she considered her options. She wrapped her hands around the post to keep herself tethered. "A few weeks ago I spotted a wild mustang on the far side of the ranch. He's the complete opposite of Duchess, white as snow. I call him Midnight Star. I want to capture him."

"What's stopping you?"

"I don't have the skill, and I'm not sure anyone else does either. At least you're gentle with the animals. I don't want any harm coming to him."

The crease in his brow deepened until it looked almost painful. "What are you hinting at?"

"I want you to come with me and help me capture him."

To her immense disappointment, he shook his head. "It's one thing to tame a horse that's already lost its freedom. I've got no interest in being the one to take away its freedom. Besides, I don't think this idea of yours would sit too well with either your father or Mitch."

She blinked in surprise. "Mitch? What does any of this have to do with him?"

"He seems to think you care for him."

She scoffed. "Well, of course I care for him. I care about a lot of the men."

Jesse suddenly scowled. "I've got work to do." He turned back to his chore.

"No one would have to know," she said quietly.

He chuckled low, a harsh sound that carried no mirth, only derision. "Yeah, that's what Sometimes-One-Eyed Pete said whenever he came up with a plan for robbing a bank."

Since her father was a judge, she knew more about the criminals of the state than did most girls her age. The law fascinated her almost as much as the man standing before her.

"Sometimes-One-Eyed Pete shot the bank teller during the last robbery, didn't he? The one where you were captured?" she asked.

He stiffened and stopped sweeping. "Yeah."

"But he managed to get away?"

"Yeah, he did." He returned to sweeping.

"Do you miss him?" she asked.

He glared at her over his shoulder. "What kind of question is that?"

She shrugged. "I just thought that maybe you were missing him."

"He wasn't my friend," he insisted. "He was my partner."

She found it interesting that he hadn't considered the bank robber his friend.

"What about the others in the gang?" she asked. "Were they your friends?"

"No. We just rode together."

More than ever, she wanted to understand not only the criminal mind, but Jesse. He'd ridden with these men, committed crimes with these men, yet he hadn't considered any of them to be friends.

"Where did you live?" she asked.

He stared at her as though he thought that if he looked at her long enough, hard enough, he could determine exactly what she was asking.

Or maybe, it occurred to her, he didn't know the answer to the question. "I mean, where was your home?"

"Beside my horse."

Now it was her turn to stare. "I mean, where was your house located? What town did you live in?"

"I lived wherever we built a fire for the night. When a posse was on our tail, I didn't even have that."

"But when you were younger, where did you live?"

Irritation clearly marking his face, he faced her squarely. His hand gripped the broom handle so tightly that his knuckles turned white.

"Where did I live when I was young? You mean after

my mother left me on somebody's doorstep? Or after I ran away from the farmer who beat me if he didn't think I worked hard enough? Or are you wanting to know where I lived after the gambler who paid me to polish his boots and fetch his whiskey got killed when someone caught him cheating?

"Or maybe you're talking about the widow who locked me in the dark closet because she was afraid I'd run away? So I did run away. And the sheriff would find me and take me back to her until I learned to run so fast and hide so well that no one could find me."

Amelia felt the tears stinging her eyes. She wasn't sure what she'd meant or what she'd been expecting. It had never occurred to her that he'd been without someone to watch over him or without a real home. She'd known he was an outlaw, but she'd never envisioned a life such as he was describing.

"Maybe you want to know about the small room where the mortician let me sleep? Wasn't much bigger than a coffin—"

"No," she said quickly, shaking her head.

"Or maybe you're interested in hearing about the store-room I slept in when the saloonkeeper wasn't making me clean up the mess that the drunks made when they got sick?"

"Stop it! Just stop it!" She spun away from him. "You're making all this up, trying to upset me."

Trying to make her feel sorry for him. She faced him and planted her hands on her hips, shoring up her resolve not to believe any of his lies.

"You went to prison when you were fourteen. No one lives with that many different people in that many years."

"They do if nobody wants them." He held her gaze for all of a heartbeat before a cold, calculating smile spread across his face. "You're right. I lied about it all. Now go back to your big house and leave me to finish my work so I can sleep in the bunkhouse tonight."

He turned his back on her and returned to sweeping. She couldn't help but believe that he hadn't lied . . . not about any of it. But based on the set of his jaw and the wounded look in his eyes, neither did she think he'd told her the whole truth.

With a desperation born of shame, Jesse shoveled out the horse droppings in the last stall. He couldn't believe he'd revealed so much about his life to Amelia. Her innocence had just irritated him.

He'd felt as though she thought everyone had the fairy-tale life she did. Everyone lived in a house with curtains fluttering in the windows and the smell of flowers wafting through the rooms. Everyone was tucked into a soft bed at night and went to sleep with a full stomach.

He'd wanted to shock her, and if the horrified expression on her face was any indication, he'd succeeded beyond his wildest dreams. But the success had left a bitter taste in his mouth. He didn't imagine Mitch Monroe ever did anything except please her.

What had possessed him to reveal all that he had?

It wasn't Amelia's fault that no one had deemed him worthy enough to love. It wasn't her fault that the widow Jones had locked him in that tiny, blackened closet. Of all the places he'd stayed, that had been the worst.

Worse than prison.

Even now it made him shudder to think of it, made him break out in a sweat. He hated small places. Part of the appeal of riding with Pete had been sleeping out beneath the stars, having the wide-open spaces as his home.

Pete had never beaten him, or yelled at him, or made him feel as though he were worthless.

Of course, none of the others had persuaded him to break the law.

He carried the last load of dung out to the field behind the barn. When he returned to the stall, he grabbed up the broom and swept out any bits that remained. As soon as he finished this chore, he'd toss down some fresh hay and be done with it.

He felt a strong urge to apologize to Amelia, but he wasn't exactly certain what specifically he was sorry for.

For not being the gentleman that her brothers were.

For thinking she was pretty when he had no right to even be looking at her.

For enjoying her conversations even though he detested the questions.

So many things.

Sometimes he felt as though his whole life was an apology.

"Ouch!" Amelia glanced down from the step stool she was standing on to glare at Colleen.

Bent slightly, her hands near Amelia's waist, Colleen looked up. "Sorry, but if you'd be still, I might have more luck at sticking the pin into the material instead of into your skin."

"I don't know why we have to do this today."

"Because your birthday dance is Saturday, and you'll be wanting to wear this new dress, won't you?" Colleen asked.

Amelia rolled her eyes, knowing what her answer would bring. "Yes."

"All right, then. I have no desire to be sewing into the wee hours of the morning just because you'd rather be out flirting with your father's ranch hands."

"I don't flirt with them," Amelia said. But her voice lacked the conviction of her words.

"And what do you call it when you smile at them, laugh with them, and talk to them every chance you get?"

"Being friendly?"

Colleen snorted, removed a pin from her waistband, and found another place to stick it in the unfinished gown Amelia was wearing. The material was a frothy green that brought out the color of her eyes and made her feel delicate. The neck was scooped low enough to show the slender column of her throat and the smoothness of her shoulders.

She'd never in her life worn anything so revealing. But then, she'd never before been seventeen and standing on the threshold of womanhood.

"I'm thinking you've got them all wrapped around your little finger," Colleen said.

All except Jesse.

"Are you going to come to my party?" Amelia asked.

"Now, why would I be wanting to do that when all the gents are only going to have eyes for you?" Colleen asked.

"Robert won't have eyes for me," Amelia said quietly, watching Colleen's reaction in the mirror.

Colleen stilled and her cheeks flamed almost as red as her hair. She angled her chin defiantly and met Amelia's gaze in the mirror. "And why would I be caring about that?"

Amelia rolled her eyes. "Admit it, Colleen. You fancy him."

"I'll admit he's not so hard on the eyes." She smiled shyly. "But I'm not certain he has much interest in me."

"Then you're not paying enough attention. He hardly takes his eyes off of you while you're serving dinner."

"That says it right there, doesn't it? He's the lord of the

manor, and I'm the serving girl. He might have an interest in giving me a kiss, but not in giving me his name. And I've no interest in a man such as that."

"I think you're wrong about Robert," Amelia said.

Colleen clapped her hands. "All done with the pinning. What do you think?"

Amelia recognized that Colleen was not only finished with the pinning, but finished with any discussion about Robert.

Amelia twisted her body first one way, then the other, studying her reflection in the mirror. The gown certainly resembled something that a young woman would wear. She pressed her hand to her bare skin just below her throat. "I've never worn anything so daring."

"I think you look lovely," Colleen said. "You'll have the men tripping over themselves to give you attention."

Strange that she suddenly couldn't stop thinking about one particular man. The one she knew she had no business getting close to.

CHAPTER ELEVEN

"I spotted the mustang again this morning."

Jesse fought to ignore the eager voice coming from behind him as he poured oats into the trough in the corral. Every time the judge's daughter approached him, he risked being sent back to prison. What did it take to make her understand he had no interest in her?

Well, that wasn't exactly true. He did have an interest in her. Too much of one. He just had no desire to go back to Huntsville.

"Did you hear what I said?" she asked.

"I heard." He shook the last of the oats out of the burlap sack.

"Don't you want to see him?" she asked.

"Not particularly." Edging past her, he headed into the barn.

She dogged his heels. "Why not?"

He spun around, and she teetered backward before catching her balance. Her eyes were so large and green, held such innocence. He could easily drown in them.

"I'm supposed to stay away from you," he reminded her.

"No one has to know. I heard Robert tell Papa this

morning that they were going to put you to work repairing the north line shack. The mustang isn't that far away from where you'll be working. I'll bring Duchess and another horse out there around midmorning. We can go see the stallion I'm interested in and be back before Tanner returns to pick you up."

It sounded simple enough. Besides, he was getting tired of looking over his shoulder and worrying that anything he did might get him sent back to prison. Five years of trying to be good was going to make him old before his time.

"If you just catch a glimpse of the horse," she said in a soft, pleading voice, "I know you'll think it's worth capturing and breaking."

"Taming," he said.

Her eyes widened. "What?"

"I tame the horse; I don't break it."

Her mouth blossomed into a radiant smile, more beautiful than any he'd ever seen her bestow on Mitch.

"So you'll do it?" she asked.

"I didn't say that."

"But you'll at least come with me and take a look?" she asked.

Gazing into eyes filled with so much hope, what choice did a fella have?

"I'll take a look," he told her, not bothering to hide his reluctance.

But she seemed unfazed by his lack of enthusiasm.

"You're going to make me the happiest girl this side of the Mississippi." She did a little hop as she turned and hurried back to the house.

He just hoped he wasn't on the verge of making himself the most miserable fella back at Huntsville.

The north line shack was exactly that—a shack. One room. Nothing fancy. Built out on the far side of nowhere.

But as Jesse replaced the planks on the roof, he thought it was a place where a man could feel at home. He wondered what it would take to convince Judge Harper to let him live here instead of in the bunkhouse.

Probably a lot more trust than the judge seemed willing to give him.

He glanced over at the smoke billowing out of the chimney. Strange how the sight added to his contentment.

Riding Starlight, Amelia had arrived earlier. As she'd promised, she'd brought a horse for Jesse. She'd announced that she was going to prepare them something to eat before they headed out to search for the mustang. Jesse had told her that she didn't need to bother. He had a bit of beef stuffed between two slices of bread that Tanner had given him to see him through the day.

She'd wrinkled up that little nose of hers and disappeared into the shack.

Leaving him to continue working up here with images dancing through his head.

The image of a hot meal in the middle of the day . . .

A girl cooking it for him . . .

A pretty girl inside the shack, cooking, while he was outside hammering a new roof into place . . .

The kind of life he'd dreamed about before prison. The kind of life he'd thought he could have if he only had enough money jangling in his pockets. The kind of life he'd thought he could purchase.

The kind of life he was beginning to realize a person had to earn.

And he'd certainly done nothing to earn it.

"Jesse!"

He gazed over his shoulder. Amelia stood away from the porch, her hand to her brow, shielding her eyes from the sun. His gut clenched. She shouldn't be here. He shouldn't be here with her.

"Are you ready to eat?" she called up.

If he were smart, he'd stay where he was and tell her he'd changed his mind. But the appeal of a meal with Amelia had him nodding and scooting toward the ladder. He stepped onto the first rung. The ladder wobbled and stilled.

He looked down. Amelia held the ladder to steady it. It was such a little thing, but still it made his chest ache.

If he wasn't careful, he was going to forget that his past prevented him from ever getting tangled up in her future.

He climbed down the ladder, his body brushing against hers as he reached the bottom. She released her hold on the ladder and quickly stepped back.

"I fried up some chicken," she said. "I thought we'd eat it over here in the shade."

She'd arranged a quilt beneath the boughs of one of the oak trees surrounding the shack.

Nodding, he rubbed his hands up and down on his britches before heading toward the quilt. He went to sit down and stopped abruptly. He remembered how he hadn't waited during the picnic that day they'd gone to Fort Worth.

He glanced over at Amelia. She gave him a shy smile and held out her hand daintily, as though she expected him to take it. He rubbed his hands on his thighs again. He wrapped his fingers around hers and helped her sit on the quilt.

Her hand was almost the softest thing he'd ever encountered—her lips the only thing softer. Even now, days later, he still remembered the gentle brush of her mouth over his cheek.

Against his browned fingers, her hand looked as pale as cream and incredibly fragile. His hand practically swallowed hers. Noticing the differences made him feel strong, and yet at the same time humble. Humble that she was inviting him to a picnic when no one else was around.

When they'd picnicked before, her brother and Colleen had been there. It hadn't seemed intimate or forbidden. But now . . .

He released her hand as though it had suddenly turned into a snake.

What was he thinking? Nothing special was going on here. She wanted him to look at a horse, and she needed to eat. That was all there was to it. Just like the picnic they'd had before. Just a chance to stop his stomach from rumbling before moving on to other things.

He dropped onto the quilt, grabbed a drumstick, and bit into the succulent meat. The more quickly they ate, the sooner they'd be on their way, and the less time he'd have to spend in her company.

Daintily, she picked up a thigh and began to nibble on the outer crust. He tossed the bones aside and reached for another piece of chicken.

"There's no posse on our trail," she said quietly.

He froze. Slowly he slid his gaze to her.

"We don't have to hurry," she explained.

"Thought you wanted to go look at that horse."

"I do, but I'm not in a big rush to do it. Do you like the chicken?"

"It's fine."

She smiled slightly. "Colleen fixed it up for me so all I had to do was drop it in the grease."

He nodded. "That was mighty thoughtful of her."

"I'm trying to convince her to come to my birthday dance."

He'd overheard some of the fellas talking about the

dance since she'd mentioned it at the corral. Everyone was anticipating dancing with Amelia.

"When we went to Fort Worth, it seemed like you were friends. Why wouldn't she go?" he asked.

She shrugged slightly, drew her knees up, and wrapped her arms around them. "We are friends. But she's fond of Robert."

Having little experience talking with females, Jesse couldn't quite figure out what one thing had to with the other. "I don't understand."

She sighed. "I think she's afraid to let Robert know how much she cares for him. Because if he knows, he'll either let her know that he cares for her as well or he'll let her know that he doesn't care for her at all. So she's afraid of getting hurt."

It still made no sense. But then love wasn't exactly an area he'd explored before.

He took a bite of chicken, chewing more slowly, savoring the flavor and the company. What would it hurt—as long as they weren't caught—if he did take his time eating?

"Does anyone know you're here?" he asked.

She slid her gaze over to him and shook her head slightly. "I trust you."

He curled his lip. "That could prove to be a big mistake."

CHAPTER TWELVE

Amelia couldn't figure out why Jesse was trying to frighten her. She wondered if he'd built a wall around his heart, and when someone started to chip away at it, he got scared.

"You won't hurt me," she announced.

"I could."

"But you won't."

Rather than confirm her suspicions, he stretched out on his side, rose up on his elbow, and picked up another piece of chicken. "Think you've got me all figured out, don't you?"

"Not really. But if you were going to hurt me, you would have done it that day at the fence."

He squinted into the distance. "Any idea how far away the Oklahoma territory is?"

"Not far enough. Besides, my brothers would find you. Papa wasn't lying when he said they were good trackers. Then you'd go back to prison. Do you prefer Huntsville?"

Silently, he shook his hanging head.

"What's it like to be in prison?" she asked. She'd asked

before, but she was hoping that this time his answer would be different.

He met her gaze. "You really don't want to know."

She was frustrated by his unwillingness to confide in her. Perhaps because he didn't feel as though she trusted him.

She set her chicken aside and wiped her greasy fingers on a towel she'd brought. She wrapped her arms tightly around her legs and rested her chin on her upraised knees.

"I've never told anyone, and I don't know why I'm telling you, but I want to practice law when I'm old enough to sit before the examination board."

He looked as though a good, strong wind would knock him flat on his back.

"A lawyer?" he asked with derision.

She nodded. "I want to represent those charged with a crime."

He barked out his laughter. "Why would you want to do that? Because you want to go up against your father?"

She furrowed her brow. "Why would you think I'd be going against my father?"

"He sends men to prison. Sounds like you want to stop them from going to prison."

"A judge doesn't send men to prison. They send themselves."

"I'm not the one who handed down a ten-year sentence—"

"But you're the one who robbed banks," she interrupted. "You can't blame a judge because you ended up in prison."

He tossed the chicken aside and wiped his hands on his britches. "We gonna go look for that horse or sit here jawin' all day?"

"I prefer to let my meal sit for a while," she lied. "So I guess we'll *jaw* for a few more minutes."

The truth was that she wanted to talk with him a little longer.

"What were you thinking while you were robbing that bank?" she asked.

"That I hoped I didn't get caught." He was staring hard at his clasped hands.

Reaching out, she trailed her finger along one of the scars on his wrist. He jerked his hand back and glared at her. She imagined that hard-edged look would have frightened just about anyone. It probably should have frightened her.

But he'd been so gentle with Duchess. A truly terrible person wouldn't treat an animal that kindly. Jesse Lawton had a spark of goodness buried somewhere inside him. She decided it was probably buried deeply, but she couldn't help but believe it was there.

Like a pearl hidden inside an oyster. Its beauty was

created from the grime at the bottom of the ocean. And Jesse's life didn't seem to have been much more than dirt and squalor.

"What were you thinking?" she prodded.

Shaking his head, he looked away.

"Were you scared?" she asked.

"Nope."

"You could have gotten killed," she pointed out.

"Didn't have anything of worth to give up," he said quietly.

"Your life—"

"Meant nothing to nobody. Not even Pete cared. Not really."

"How did you meet him?" she asked.

A corner of his mouth quirked up. "You remember that mortician I told you about?"

"The one you lived with for a while?" she asked.

"Yep, that's the one. He was teaching me to prepare the bodies for burial."

She shivered with the thought of being around corpses. She knew someone had to do the grisly task, but she'd certainly never contemplated taking it on.

"Well, they'd hanged Pete that morning—"

"They'd hanged him?" she blurted out.

The corner of his mouth rose a little higher. "Yep. They'd caught him stealing a horse. Steal money and you go to prison. Steal a horse and they hang you. No trial. No courtroom. Just the nearest tree and a long length of strong rope.

"Anyway, they'd dumped him on the table and told me to get him ready for his pine box. It was just him and me in that dimly lit room. He was the first dead person I'd ever spent much time around, and he made the hairs on the back of my neck stand on end."

She could well imagine that he had. Just hearing about it had the fine hairs on the nape of her neck prickling.

"I went to button his collar. Didn't think he ought to meet his maker with the rope burn showing, and he grabbed my arm."

"I would have swooned," she said. "After I'd hollered."

His slight smile revealed his perfect teeth. "I was too startled to do much of anything but stare. Pete just grinned. Said he had nine lives, just like a cat. He asked me to help him escape. I figured he deserved to get away, fooling the Grim Reaper like he did. I hid him at the train depot and bought him a ticket. When he invited me to come along"—he shrugged—"I went. I'd never had anybody ask me to join them on an adventure."

He shook his head. "Some adventure."

He started picking at some loose threads in the quilt as though embarrassed that he'd revealed so much.

"Why didn't you leave when you learned he was robbing banks?" she asked.

"He said those folks didn't need the money. We did."

"Whether or not they needed it wasn't the point. They'd earned it and the right to keep it."

He lifted his gaze then, a yearning for understanding reflected in his eyes. "I was twelve. I'd never had anyone tell me that I'd done a good job. I'd never had anybody *need* me. Pete needed me, and I was good at climbing up to the roof, where I could reach an open window on the second floor or slip down a chimney. I'd open the door for Pete. He taught me how to open a safe. He said I was a natural. His words made me feel good. Don't know if I'd ever felt good about myself."

Amelia had never before been so confused. She couldn't condone what he'd done. She wasn't even certain she could comprehend the reasons that he'd done it. What she did understand was that Jesse had grown up with no love and little praise.

"Stop looking at me like that," he snapped. "I didn't tell you that story so you'd pity me."

"I don't pity you," she shot back.

Although her heart did go out to him. But if he was anything like her contrary brothers, he had an abundance of pride. "I think you were a fool to blindly follow Pete."

"That's the gosh-darned truth. I won't fall for false praise again, I can promise you that."

Amelia was beginning to realize that she'd had a very sheltered life. No one had broken her heart; no one had ever shattered her trust.

And yet here she was sitting on a quilt with a young man whose life had been the complete opposite of hers. She'd thought listening to his tale would satisfy her curiosity about him. All it had done was convince her that she wanted to know more.

"What will you do when you've finished serving your time?" she asked quietly.

Releasing a deep sigh, he sat up. "Haven't thought that far ahead. Right now it's all I can do to get through one day without bolting."

"You mean you think about escaping?" she asked stunned.

"All the time."

"But this isn't a prison."

"It doesn't have walls or locked doors. But for me, Amelia, it's still prison. No one trusts me enough to leave me a horse."

She heard the disappointment reflected in his voice. But more, she saw the humiliation swimming within his eyes. Just as it had been when he'd stepped off the train at the depot and his shackles had clanged around him.

Just as it had been when she'd approached him in the corral, and he'd known that her need to uphold her end of the promise had brought her lips to his cheek instead of to his mouth.

She wanted him to help her capture the mustang, but so much more was involved. She couldn't explain it—

he haunted her thoughts, invaded her dreams. Images bombarded her—Jesse skirting the edge of a crowd or standing at the fringes of a group of men.

Loneliness. She suddenly realized what it was she was seeing when she looked at him. A shroud of loneliness.

Unexpectedly she felt mean-spirited and trivial for not being willing to offer to him what she would have offered to any other cowboy who had tamed Duchess for her.

Slowly she leaned toward him in the same manner that a moth was drawn to a flickering flame, hovering near, knowing even as it approached that it risked getting burned.

The lines in Jesse's face ran deep, carved by hardship and sorrow.

Her heart tightened into a painful knot as she considered all he might have suffered.

She saw fear suddenly flare within his eyes.

"Don't," he rasped.

"I owe you a proper kiss for taming Duchess," she whispered.

He shook his head slightly, but he didn't move out of harm's way, and she wondered if he was as powerless to prevent what was coming as she was.

Closing her eyes, she pressed her lips to his.

While he'd seemed hesitant, now that she'd committed them to a kiss, he wasn't tentative at all.

He kissed her as though his life depended on it.

But for all his enthusiasm, she sensed that he was

holding back much more. She knew he'd received no comfort in prison, and based upon what he'd revealed in the barn, she thought he might never have received any.

He cradled her cheek with one hand, the gentlest touch she'd ever felt. With his thumb, he slowly stroked her cheek and gentled the kiss. She wrapped her arm around his neck and ran her fingers up into his thick hair.

He drew back, and she saw confusion swimming in his blue eyes.

"Shouldn't have done that," he said in a voice that sounded like sandpaper rubbed against coarse wood.

"I shouldn't have kissed you? Or you shouldn't have kissed me back?"

"Both. Amelia, you don't want to get tangled up with the likes of me."

She eased back, furrowing her brow. "I don't think you're as bad as you think you are, Jesse Lawton."

"Are we going to go look for that mustang?" he asked brusquely, as though he feared treading the path she was starting down.

She smiled softly. He intrigued her more than he should. But she knew he wasn't nearly as tough on the inside as he was on the outside. "You get the horses while I put the picnic away."

If anyone had ever told Jesse that he'd kiss a judge's daughter—and be grateful that he had—he would have called the man a fool.

Instead he was calling himself a fool as he rode beside her.

Whenever he was around her, he'd begin to think that maybe, maybe after he'd served his time, he might have a chance at a normal life. She spoke to him as though she cared about what he had to say. No one had ever done that. Not even Pete.

He was beginning to understand why every cowboy had been willing to risk a broken bone to gain her favor by breaking Duchess. She had a way of looking at him and making him feel as though no one else in the world was as important.

He told himself she was just doing it so she could convince him to help her capture that mustang she wanted.

Still, he couldn't forget the softness of her cheek or the tenderness of her kiss.

His mind kept coming back to that kiss. She'd tasted so sweet. Once when the widow had been in a good mood, she'd allowed him to lick the spoon she'd used to whip up the icing she'd spread over a cake. Amelia was better than sugared icing.

She glanced over at him and smiled. It irritated him that he thought he might do just about anything to have that smile aimed his way. Yet at the same time, it pleased him to see it.

"Have you always had a way with animals?" she asked.

He couldn't quite get used to her interest in him, couldn't recall ever carrying on what he'd consider a real conversation. The most talking he'd ever done involved understanding exactly what he was supposed to do during the bank robberies.

He nodded. "Best as I can recollect."

"They're not as judgmental as people," she said softly.

"That's true."

"How will you capture the mustang?"

He shook his head. "Didn't say I would."

"But if you were going to?"

"Slow and easy. He's probably got a herd of mares somewhere," he said. "Have you ever seen them?"

"No. I've seen him on that ridge in the distance."

He squinted at the rising slope of ground. Trees and brush lined the ridge and dotted the land spreading out before them. There wasn't anyplace for a man to hide.

"I'm not really interested in the mares," she said, interrupting his thoughts.

"It would be easier to approach him, though, and get him to trust me if I could ease my way into the herd. If it's just him and me, then it'll be harder."

"I'll race you to the rise," she suddenly announced.

Before he could respond, she'd nudged Duchess's flanks and sent the mare into a gallop. He kicked his own horse, urging him to follow.

Without warning, her horse released a high-pitched

neigh and reared up, its front legs churning in the air.

Amelia screamed.

The horse bucked wildly.

Amelia flew out of the saddle and landed hard on the ground.

Jesse galloped to where Amelia had fallen. Pulling back on the reins, he leaped off his horse before it came to a stop. He knelt beside Amelia.

She was as still as death.

His heart was thundering as loudly as the horse's hooves had just moments before.

"Amelia?"

Leaning over her, he touched her cheek. He was afraid to move her, afraid to do anything that might hurt her more than she was already hurt. Looking closely, he could see a thin trail of blood along the back of her neck. She must have hit her head on a rock when she'd fallen.

Or had the horse kicked her? It had all happened so quickly that he wasn't sure.

He heard a rumble in the distance. Looking over his shoulder, he saw a group of riders. A plume of dust billowed up behind them.

He recognized the two lead riders as they brought their horses to a halt: her brothers. Several other men were with them.

Thank goodness. They could help him get Amelia back to the house.

Robert and David quickly dismounted.

"She's hurt," Jesse said. "I don't know——"

David grabbed him by the shirt and jerked him to his feet. Then he plowed his fist into Jesse's stomach. The air whooshed out of him as he dropped to his knees. He wanted to explain what had happened, but without the ability to draw a breath——

"You son of a . . ." David growled as he punched Jesse in the jaw.

Stars flashed before Jesse's eyes as he hit the ground. He looked toward Amelia. Dark shadows hovered at the edge of his vision. He could see Robert lifting her limp body.

Someone pulled him to his feet. Mitch. He hit Jesse harder than he'd ever been hit in his life.

Without the ability to draw in air, he couldn't talk. But he quickly realized it didn't matter. They wouldn't believe anything he had to say anyway.

CHAPTER THIRTEEN

Amelia's head felt like a herd of wild mustangs was stampeding through it. Slowly she opened her eyes. She was lying in her bed in her dimly lit bedroom. How had she gotten here?

With concern etched on his face, her father sat on the edge of her bed. "How many fingers am I holding up?" he asked.

She smiled at his silly question. "Three."

She started to lift her head, but pain throbbed at the base of her skull. Moaning, she placed her hand at the back of her head and became aware of the bandage.

"What happened?" she asked.

"You were attacked," Robert said.

She shifted her gaze slightly and saw her brothers standing at the foot of her bed. Colleen was with them. She'd never seen them looking as worried as they appeared to be now.

"Attacked?" she repeated, trying to make sense of his words.

"We saw smoke coming from the area of the north line shack," David said. "We couldn't figure out why there would be any. We thought maybe the building or a section of grass had caught fire. We got to the shack and saw tracks, so we followed them. We caught up with Jesse before he was able to hurt you any more than he already had."

She furrowed her brow. For heaven's sake. What was her brother blabbering about?

"Hurt me? Jesse?"

"He had you on the ground, Amelia," Robert said. "Unconscious. We saw him leaning over you."

Everything started rushing through her mind like a storm encroaching on the land. Sitting up quickly, she grabbed her head to try to stifle the pain.

Her father gently put his hands on her shoulders. "Lie back down, sweetheart. You're safe here. He'll never bother you again."

Her stomach tightened. Despite the anticipated pain, she shook her head. "No, Jesse didn't attack me."

"Amelia, we saw him," David told her.

"I don't know what you saw. We were riding, and Duchess suddenly reared up . . . a snake. She saw a rattler. I remember now. I lost my seating and tumbled off. Didn't he tell you that?"

Robert shifted his stance, and David lowered his gaze to his boots, both suddenly looking extremely uncomfortable.

"I'm thinking they didn't give him much of a chance to

say anything," Colleen said.

"You didn't even ask him what happened?" Amelia asked.

David shook his head. "We had several men with us. They all thought the same thing we did."

"What were we supposed to think? I know he made you cry the day we took him to Fort Worth for clothes," Robert said.

"What's this?" her father asked suspiciously. "Why am I just now hearing about this?"

"He didn't *make* me cry," she rushed to explain.

Why was everything getting blown so far out of proportion? She might have laughed if her head weren't hurting so badly.

"Amelia, I saw the tears," Robert insisted.

"I thought I'd been brazen when I purchased a dime novel—went against Papa's wishes. You know that he doesn't approve of my reading them. When I showed the book to Jesse, he laughed. He didn't think I'd been bad at all.

"I let his laughter hurt my feelings, and like a ninny I got all weepy. That's all. He didn't do anything he shouldn't have done that day. And he didn't do anything wrong today."

"We didn't know that," Robert said. "We just assumed . . ."

"You assumed what?" she demanded.

"The worst," he said quietly.

Something was wrong; something was horribly wrong. She could tell by the way that David refused to look at her and continued to hang his head, as he'd done when he was a little boy and gotten into trouble.

Steal a horse and they hang you, Jesse had said. Had they thought he'd stolen the horse he'd been riding?

"Where's Jesse?" she asked, unable to keep the panic out of her voice.

"We locked him in the back room in the barn. Figured to take him back to the depot and on to Huntsville tomorrow," Robert said.

"No!" Amelia flung back the covers and scrambled out of bed despite the racking pain in her head. "He didn't do anything wrong. If anyone did, it was me. I took him a horse; I invited him to come with me."

"Amelia, you shouldn't get out of bed," Colleen said.

"I'm fine. I want to see Jesse." She turned to her father. "Papa, he didn't want me to be with him. He didn't want to break your rules. I was the one who disobeyed. Please let me see him."

Her father narrowed his eyes and looked at her brothers. "I think I'd like to see him, too."

As long as he kept his eyes closed, Jesse could pretend that he wasn't locked in a tiny dark room. He could pretend he was outside on a moonless night. A night thick with clouds that stopped the stars from shining though. A still night with no breeze. Just stifling heat.

As long as he kept his jaw clamped shut, he couldn't scream.

When he was a little boy and the widow had locked him in a closet beneath the stairs, he'd cried until he had no more tears and yelled until his throat was raw.

Neither action had helped him then. He didn't think much was going to help him now.

He ached in more places than he knew he had. Mitch had delivered a second blow that had knocked him out. He'd awoken to find himself here, in the dark. He'd noticed a small empty room in the barn when he'd hauled feed to the horses. So he figured that was where he was. They'd probably used it for storage at some point. Now they were using it as his cell.

He was worried about Amelia, but he figured since they hadn't hanged him yet she was still alive. He just wished she'd wake up and be all right.

He knew they'd send him back to prison. Caught on the prairie with a horse and the judge's daughter . . . He'd seen the hatred and distrust in her brothers' eyes.

He never should have accepted Judge Harper's offer. He should have simply stayed in prison. Served out his time there. Going back was going to be much harder because now he possessed something he hadn't before— the memory of Amelia.

He'd been foolish to begin thinking that everything

would be all right—that he was just like everyone else.

They'd seen Amelia lying there and had drawn their own conclusions without even bothering to ask him what had happened. His past was always going to dog his heels. No one would ever trust him.

He heard a key being inserted into a lock, followed by the harsh grinding sound as it was turned. The door swung open. He squinted against the light spilling in from the lantern that someone held.

"Oh, my goodness, just look at you!"

Amelia's sweet voice echoed around him. She knelt beside him and gently lifted his hair off his brow.

"Oh, look what they've done to you."

"Are you all right?" he rasped.

He certainly hadn't expected Judge Harper to let her get within a whisper's breath of him.

"I must have hit my head when I fell. Robert, help him get up," she ordered.

"I don't need help," he said as he struggled to his feet. As long as he didn't take a deep breath, the pain was bearable.

"You are so stubborn," she muttered as she took his arm. "Come on. Let's get you into the house."

He froze. "What?"

"We need to get you into the house so I can see to your injuries," she said.

"I'm fine."

"Well, then, it won't take me long to check you out, will it?"

Facing prison was going to be hard enough as it was. He didn't need any more memories of her sweetness to take with him.

"Look, Amelia—"

"Don't argue with her, son." Judge Harper's voice boomed around him. He hadn't even realized the man was standing there. "Get on up to the house."

He considered arguing, but the sooner he did what they wanted, the sooner he'd be on his way. He expected the judge to order his daughter to loosen her hold on the outlaw, but the man simply followed behind them as Amelia led him toward the house.

That her brothers were trailing behind didn't make him feel any less watched.

Once they were inside, he'd expected to turn in to the judge's library. Instead Amelia escorted him farther into the house—past a parlor and a room that held a large table with a fancy-looking candleholder on it.

Amelia pushed open a door, and they walked into the kitchen. Colleen stood beside the stove. She turned and her mouth dropped open.

"Don't look like that, Colleen," Robert said from behind him. "I didn't hit him."

"I should hope not." She wagged a finger in the air. "And you, David Harper, should be ashamed of yourself."

"Sit here," Amelia said as she pulled out a chair from a nearby table.

He hadn't a clue why they needed two tables to eat at—one in this room, one in the other—but he figured wealthy folks were always purchasing things they didn't need. He sat, and Colleen set a bowl of water on the table.

"I'll tend to him," Amelia said as she took a chair and sat in front of him.

He really thought it was a waste of her time to clean him up when the cuts would just get dirty again in prison. But he figured arguing would simply prolong the inevitable.

She dipped a rag into the bowl, wrung it out, and gingerly touched the warm, damp cloth to his brow. Even though it stung, he thought he'd never forget the night he sat in this kitchen that smelled of cinnamon and had the prettiest girl he'd ever seen tending to his cuts and bruises.

He couldn't stop himself from watching her. She'd furrowed her brow and caught her lower lip between her teeth as she carefully wiped the blood and dirt from his face. He could see tears welling in her eyes.

"It's not that bad," he said in a low voice, wishing they didn't have an audience.

She held his gaze as more tears surfaced. "You're going to have a blackened eye come morning."

"Just one?" he asked, trying to make light of his injuries.

She gave him a tremulous smile as she cradled his

cheek in her palm. "I am so sorry."

In his whole life, he couldn't recall anyone ever apologizing to him. He couldn't quite figure out what he was supposed to say.

"All right. Everybody out," Judge Harper demanded.

Jesse shot to his feet, sucking in air through his clenched teeth as pain stabbed his chest.

"Not you," Judge Harper said to him, his eyes narrowing. "I was talking to my sons. You can sit back down."

Jesse did as he was told while Robert and David left the room.

Judge Harper crouched beside him. It was an odd thing to be looking down at the judge. With a gentleness that Jesse never would have expected of such a large man, Judge Harper prodded Jesse's ribs.

Jesse held his breath, waiting for the pain to pass.

"Feels like a couple might be cracked, possibly broken," Judge Harper announced, as though Jesse hadn't already figured that out.

"I'll get some strips of cloth so we can bind his chest to keep those ribs from moving until they heal," Colleen said.

"Anything else broken?" Judge Harper asked.

"No, sir."

Judge Harper nodded as he stood. "Then I'll leave you to these ladies' tender mercies while I have a little chat with the men and make sure they understand that nothing like this is to ever happen again."

Judge Harper strode out of the kitchen.

Jesse shifted his gaze to Amelia. "He's not sending me back to Huntsville?"

She smiled softly. "He knows the truth. I told him that I wanted you to help me capture the mustang. How Duchess saw the rattler—"

"There was a snake?" he asked. He hadn't seen one, but he knew they could slither away quickly.

She nodded.

He released a slow breath of relief. "I was afraid I hadn't tamed her enough, and she was turning back to the wild."

"No, she was just frightened. Frank found her and brought her back. Take off your shirt so I can see your ribs."

Slowly he unbuttoned his shirt and opened it slightly. She gasped. Without looking, he knew what she was seeing. Based on the way his body ached, he figured he was black and blue pretty much all over.

She touched her trembling hand to her lips as tears flooded her eyes. Tears for him.

He had to steel his heart against Amelia. She was more dangerous to him than any outlaw gang had ever been.

CHAPTER FOURTEEN

"For more than twenty years, I've been involved with the law."

Her father's solemn voice echoed through his library with disappointment. After speaking with the men, he was now holding a meeting with her, her brothers, Colleen, and Tanner. Amelia had expected to be in trouble for purposely seeking Jesse out earlier that day, but it seemed her brothers' transgressions far outweighed hers.

"In all that time," her father continued, "I never perpetuated the kind of injustice I've witnessed today. By my own sons, no less."

"But, Father," David began.

"A man is innocent until proven guilty," her father interrupted.

"We thought we were looking at the proof," Robert stated firmly.

"Well, you were wrong, weren't you?" her father asked.

"Papa, what did you expect from them or the cowhands when you've made them all expect the worst of Jesse?" Amelia asked quietly.

He snapped his gaze around to her, and she almost

wished she'd remained silent. But she'd been horrified when she'd seen the bruises on Jesse's battered body.

"I did not make them expect the worst of Jesse," her father said in a voice that indicated he'd brook no argument.

She'd grown up with that voice and had always assumed he knew best. But if she truly planned to practice law, she was going to have to learn to stand up in a courtroom and state her case. Might as well begin with this judge as with any other.

She slowly rose and met his gaze squarely. "We all heard you set down a host of rules for him to follow. I don't know how he can draw a breath without fearing that he's broken one."

"The boy has to earn his freedom," her father said.

"But you're making him feel as though he's worthless. You don't trust him to do as he's told. You don't trust him not to run off. Tanner takes him to the fence to work or the line shack, and then leaves him there alone and without a horse—"

"Whoa!" Tanner cut in. "I'll admit to leaving him at the north line shack by himself, but I didn't leave him alone at the fence. What makes you think I did?"

She was likely to get herself into trouble if she revealed that today wasn't the first time she'd been alone with Jesse, but what he said made no sense. "I was riding out in that direction and saw him working on the fence. He was alone."

Tanner shook his head. "I left Mitch and Frank with him."

"They weren't there. He was stringing the wire by himself," she insisted.

"I'm willing to bet that they took off for the swimming hole," David said.

"And Jesse was working when you saw him?" Tanner asked her.

"He said you told him that it needed to be done."

"So you approached him and talked to him," her father said, and she heard the censure in his voice.

She was going to have to learn not to give away so much upon cross-examination.

"He didn't hurt me. As a matter of fact, anytime I talk to him, he reminds me that I'm not supposed to be anywhere near him," she said.

She stepped forward, placed her palms on his desk, and leaned toward him. "No one has ever given him a chance to be anything but bad. I know he was wrong to rob a bank, but I don't think he's a terrible person. He could have ridden away from me today, but he didn't."

She took a deep breath before confessing, "I spent over an hour with him at the line shack, and he showed me nothing but respect."

She could see the fury boiling within her father's eyes, but he kept his voice steady. "All right. Tanner, you treat him as you treat the other hands—within reason. You can leave a horse with him, but not a gun. This meeting is adjourned."

Smiling, she spun on her heels.

"Amelia?"

She looked back at her father.

"If you pull what you did today—purposely disobeying me and spending time alone with Jesse—I'll send him back from where he came."

"You can't punish him for my actions," she said, angered by the very thought of it.

"I can. I'm your father. I expect Jesse to follow my rules, and I expect you to follow them as well."

She knew that she'd never made her father this angry before. Growing up was like walking a fine line, and she didn't much like it. But she did live under his roof.

She nodded curtly. "Yes, sir."

She walked out of the room with her head held high, realizing her father's order would stop her from ever capturing the mustang she wanted.

But more, it would stop her from getting to know Jesse Lawton better.

And she desperately wanted to know him better.

Jesse had felt strange walking into the bunkhouse.

Whereas before everyone had narrowed their eyes at

him, now they all seemed more interested in the knotholes in the walls than they were in him.

Which suited him just fine as he lay on his bed staring at the ceiling.

It had hurt to hoist himself up, but as he'd told Amelia, he'd suffered worse.

He needed to stop thinking about her. Every time he closed his eyes, he saw her clearly. It was like her image had been branded onto his mind. He couldn't seem to forget her gentle touch or the concern in her eyes.

The men were still awake. Some played cards. Some read. Others were writing letters. Jesse thought that after his time here was over and he'd moved on, maybe he'd write a letter to Amelia. Just to thank her for . . . well, pretty much everything.

He heard footsteps.

"I warned you to stay away from Amelia," Mitch said in a low, menacing voice.

Jesse didn't bother to look at the man.

"Someday you're gonna regret hitting me as hard as you did," Jesse told him.

"Are you threatening me, outlaw?"

"If I was, you wouldn't have to ask," Jesse assured him.

The door opened, and Tanner strode in. "Jesse!"

Mitch scuttled away like the cockroach Jesse was beginning to associate with the man.

Tanner jerked a thumb over his shoulder. "Amelia

wants to have a word with you outside."

Jesse threw his legs over the side of the bed and hopped down. His body screamed at the abuse, but he didn't give in to the pain. Not with every man in the bunkhouse watching him.

He could feel Mitch's gaze drilling into his back as he strode to the door.

He stepped outside. Amelia stood near the porch with Robert nearby—close enough to protect her, but not close enough to hear.

She gave Jesse a timid smile. "Sit down."

She indicated the porch. Jesse dropped to the top step. She sat beside him.

"Are you hurting?" she asked softly.

It seemed an odd question. It had been only an hour or so since he'd walked out of her house.

"Not as much."

"I just wanted you to know . . ." Her voice trailed off as she gazed down at her hands. She sighed. "My father is very upset."

His gut clenched. "So he's changed his mind? He's sending me back?"

She lifted her gaze to him and smiled. "No. But he's forbidden me to spend any time with you if someone isn't around."

"He did that before, and it didn't stop you," he reminded her.

"I know. But tonight he was using his 'I am your father' voice. It's a subtle difference, but it means he absolutely will not tolerate me disobeying his orders on this matter."

He nodded.

"I just wanted you to know . . . I didn't want you to think that I was ignoring you if I don't talk to you or seek you out like I have before. I really don't want him to send you back to prison."

He didn't want that to happen either.

She stood. "Good night."

Watching her walk away, Jesse slowly came to his feet.

Robert approached. "Reckon I owe you an apology for what happened today. I should have stopped them from beating on you."

Yeah, you should have, Jesse thought. On the other hand, he might have allowed the same thing to happen if he'd had any suspicions that someone might have hurt Amelia.

"Let's just forget it happened," he suggested.

Amelia sat in a chair beside the window in her bedroom and gazed out at the moon.

How could she miss Jesse?

It made no sense to her. She couldn't stop thinking about him. She couldn't forget his kiss.

She turned her head at the gentle knock on her door. "Come in."

Colleen slipped inside, the green gown draped over her arm.

"Well, I finished it." She held it up. "I think it turned out lovely."

"It's beautiful," Amelia said.

Colleen laid it across the bed before walking around and sitting on the bed so she was closer to Amelia. "I thought you might be needing to talk."

With a sigh, Amelia looked back at the night. "I'm so confused, Colleen."

"In what way?"

"I think Mitch is good-looking. And Frank is always smiling. And every man in that bunkhouse is dependable. And everyone is coming to my party. But I don't want to dance with a single one of them."

"That's because you took a blow to the head and it knocked the good sense out of you," Colleen said smartly.

Amelia peered over at her. Trust Colleen not to allow her to feel sorry for herself for very long.

"Oh, Colleen." Amelia went to the bed and sat beside her friend. "I don't know what's wrong with me. I'm only a few days away from being seventeen. I've been waiting forever to have a sweetheart. And the one fella I suddenly find myself interested in is the wrong one for me. Oh, I don't know!"

She flopped back on the bed and stared at the canopy over it.

"I mean, Jesse has certainly never indicated that he has any feelings for me whatsoever. 'Stay away from me.' 'Don't talk to me.' 'You'll get me sent back to prison.' I don't know if he says all those things because he fears going back to prison or he fears what caring for me might bring."

"He probably doesn't know either. Men are not the brightest creatures on God's green earth," Colleen said.

Smiling, Amelia looked at her. "You don't have a very high opinion of men."

"I adore them," Colleen admitted. "But they're frustrating."

"Will you come to my party?"

Colleen shook her head. "There will be girls from town wanting to dance with Robert."

"And he just wants to dance with you."

"I don't know if I want to go to the dance, Amelia. You don't know if Jesse is right for you because he's an outlaw. I don't know if I'm right for Robert because I'm a servant," Colleen said.

"I'm not sure we should judge ourselves or other people by what we or they are," Amelia said quietly.

She thought about the different times she'd been with Jesse: in Fort Worth, at the fence, at the north line shack.

If she'd never had any time with him, she wouldn't have this warm feeling curling inside of her now whenever she thought of him.

He'd still simply be the outlaw who'd stepped off the train.

Instead of the young man who was slowly stealing her heart.

CHAPTER FIFTEEN

Jesse held the barbed wire taut while Frank hammered the U-shaped nail into place against the post they'd recently placed in the ground. With all the land Judge Harper owned, Jesse figured he'd be planting posts and stringing wire as long as he remained at the ranch.

Amelia had been right, though: it was easier to build a fence when he had someone to help him.

Frank finished slamming the nail into place and stepped back. He tipped his hat off his brow and glanced over at the man lounging beneath the tree.

"You know, Mitch, we could get this job done a lot quicker if you'd help us," Frank said.

"I don't work beside outlaws, especially when they're tattletales," Mitch ground out.

Jesse pulled the wire over to the next post. He knew Mitch was blaming him because Tanner had warned Mitch and Frank that they were to stay put. He knew it had irritated Mitch that Tanner hadn't given the same instruction to Jesse.

Jesse was still having a difficult time believing that Tanner had left him a horse.

Frank positioned the nail.

"I didn't tell Tanner about the two of you going swimming," Jesse said quietly.

He couldn't figure out why he cared what they thought. Maybe he was just getting tired of being accused of things that weren't his fault.

Frank glared at him. "Then who did? You're the only one who knew."

Jesse shook his head. "I don't know how Tanner found out. I didn't say anything to anyone. It's none of my business if you take off."

"But it's our business if you do," Frank told him. He hammered the nail.

Bang.

"Tanner told us to keep an eye on you that first day."

Bang.

"So it was more than just not working on the fence that got us in trouble. It was not staying where we were supposed to."

Bang.

Frank straightened. "So why didn't you run?"

Jesse strung the wire over to the next post. Frank tagged along like a puppy nipping at his heels.

"How come you didn't take off?" Frank repeated.

Jesse held his gaze. "Wasn't willing to risk getting sent back to prison. Nothing in this world is worse than prison. And that's a fact."

"Mitch bet me two bits that you'd run. Think it aggravates him some that he keeps guessing wrong where you're concerned. Although he made me pay him back the quarter he lost on that bet we made about you tattling on us to Tanner—since he figured you did it."

"Well, he's wrong, so he owes you that money," Jesse said.

Frank grinned and held out the hammer. "You want to do some hammering for a while?"

"Reckon."

Jesse took the tool and waited while Frank stretched the wire taut and held it in place. He brought his arm back.

"Did you see Amelia—"

Jesse swung.

"Yeow!" Frank yelled as he jumped back, holding his hand.

Jesse swore beneath his breath. No cussing, Judge Harper had said.

But hearing Amelia's name had distracted him, changed his focus. He'd stopped looking at the nail and jerked his head around, halfway expecting to see Amelia riding up.

Mitch started laughing.

"Are you hurt?" Jesse asked, knowing the question was stupid but not knowing what else to say.

"Of course he's hurt," Mitch said. "Why do you think he's hollering?"

Frank flicked his hand. "Nah, I'm all right."

"You idiot. Don't you know better than to trust him?" Mitch asked.

Jesse clenched his teeth to keep his anger from erupting. No fighting, Judge Harper had said. But if ever there was a man who needed hitting, Jesse figured it was Mitch.

Jesse held the hammer out toward Frank. "Maybe you'd better do the hitting."

"Nah," Frank said as he grabbed the barbed wire. "Accidents happen. I shouldn't have distracted you with talking. I was just wondering if you saw the notice Amelia posted outside the bunkhouse about the dance this Saturday night."

Jesse moved in closer to the post. "Yeah, I saw it."

"You going?"

"He's not invited," Mitch said.

Frank glanced over at him. "The invitation said for everyone."

Mitch unfolded his body and strolled lazily toward the fence. He stopped a few inches away from Jesse and held his gaze. "The invitation didn't include you."

"Didn't think it did," Jesse ground out.

This time when he swung the hammer, he embedded the nail into the post with only one strike.

"Make the bow just a tad fuller!" Colleen called up to Jesse as he crouched in the barn loft.

A tad fuller? A bow was a bow, as far as Jesse was

concerned, but this bossy lady was acting as though it were a matter of life or death if Jesse didn't do the thing just right. He didn't understand why they needed to fancy the barn up anyway. The dance was taking place in the main house.

Today Tanner had ordered him to be at the ladies' beck and call while they were getting things ready for Amelia's birthday celebration. He couldn't believe all the fussing going on.

Of course, he didn't even know when his birthday was, and he was certain no one had ever celebrated his birth.

Kneeling in the loft, though, he struggled to make the bow fuller, but the looped portions just sort of drooped down.

"Have you no idea how to tie a proper bow then?" Colleen asked.

She had a funny way of talking that made Jesse sort of grin inside.

But she didn't make him smile inside as much as Amelia did. Ever since the day of misunderstanding—as Tanner and her brothers referred to it—Amelia hadn't approached him while he was working alone.

Sometimes he'd spot her watching him, but she didn't come over and talk to him. Today was probably the first time that he'd actually spent any time with her. And that was only because she was helping Colleen in the barn.

He'd taken the animals out to pasture earlier and then

cleaned out the stalls. He'd laid down fresh straw. And now he was doing this decorating thing. And not doing a very good job of it, if the way the ladies were snickering was any indication.

He shook his head. "It's just a bow."

"But it looks sad," Colleen shouted up. "It's supposed to look happy."

"Happy? How can a bow look happy?" he called down. They wanted him to hang bows around all the posts supporting the roof. At this rate he'd be here come evening. And he definitely wanted to be gone long before then—before the guests started arriving.

In the bunkhouse, he'd overheard the men talking about this event all week. Tonight was the big night, Amelia's seventeenth birthday. After tonight she could officially begin entertaining suitors.

Amelia's laughter echoed around the barn. "I'll show you."

He watched her march toward the ladder that led into the loft. His heart started hammering as she climbed up. He wrapped his hands around the ladder to steady it. If he were smart, he'd tell her to head back down.

Instead as she climbed into the loft, he scuttled back.

She gave him an impish smile. "My brothers can't tie a decent bow either."

Leaning over slightly, she slipped her arms around the beam and went to work at undoing the mess he'd created with the strip of red silk.

"How does that look, Colleen?" she asked.

"Perfect, lass. Maybe you'd best do the others as well since you're up there."

"All right." Clapping her hands together, Amelia settled back on her heels.

"Reckon you don't need me up here if you're going to do the decorating," he said.

"Don't go," she pleaded softly. "Colleen's down there working, so we're not really alone."

She took a length of silk from the pile he'd brought up earlier and ran it through her slender fingers. "I guess it's silly to decorate the barn, but I'm sure a few people will wander outside for a walk. And if anyone brings their children, they'll probably play out here."

She peered over at him. "How are your ribs?"

"Getting better."

Reaching out, she trailed her fingers over his cheek, down along his chin. He nearly forgot to breathe.

"Your bruises are fading."

He thought maybe he should say something, but for the life of him he couldn't think of anything to say.

"Are you going to come to the dance this evening?" she asked.

"Wasn't planning on it."

With the sunlight spilling through the opening in the loft, he was able to see the disappointment cross her face.

"I wish you would."

"You're gonna have plenty of attention tonight. You don't need me there."

"But I *want* you there."

He shook his head. "I have no interest in coming."

"Hey, my beauty!"

Amelia's eyes widened. "That's Robert!" she whispered.

With a sly smile, she pressed a finger to her mouth. She eased farther back until she was close enough to Jesse that he'd only have to turn his head to brush his lips over her cheek. He couldn't believe how incredibly tempting the realization was.

"And what would you be wanting now, with all that sweet talk, I'd like to know?" Colleen's voice drifted up through the rafters.

"Amelia tells me that you're not coming to the dance tonight."

"That's right; I'm not."

"Come here," he commanded in a voice filled with persuasion. "I'll convince you that you want to be there."

"Robert, we're not—"

Jesse had a feeling Colleen had been about to inform Robert that they weren't alone. Amelia leaned into him.

"I think he's kissing her." Her face was bathed in sunshine, her smile bright. "I knew they liked each other."

"Robert! I'm trying to tell you—" Colleen began, then fell back into silence.

Jesse could only assume Robert was kissing her again. He remembered the kiss he'd shared with Amelia.

His thoughts must have shown on his face, because her mouth shifted from a smile into an invitation. He couldn't say exactly what the difference was, but he was certain it was there.

He cradled her chin and stroked his thumb over her lower lip. It was so soft. Her breath warmed his skin.

He slowly lowered his mouth—

"What!" Robert suddenly yelled.

Jesse jerked back. Amelia looked as disappointed as he was that he hadn't reached his destination.

"Amelia, are you up there?" Robert called out.

She grimaced, moved to the edge of the loft, and fluttered the silk in the air. "I'm making bows. Don't pay any attention to me. Just go back to your kissing."

He glared at her. "Are you up there alone?"

"Not exactly."

"Jesse!" Robert yelled.

Jesse scooted over so he could look down into the barn. Robert had a voice almost as booming as his father's.

"I trust both of you to keep my little indiscretion to yourselves," Robert ordered.

Colleen planted her hands on her hips. "Indiscretion, am I?"

She shoved him before storming toward the door.

"That's not what I meant," Robert called after her retreating back. "Colleen?"

Shaking his head, he looked up at the loft. "Now look what you did."

Amelia's eyes widened. "Me? I didn't do anything. You're the one who hurt her feelings. Go apologize."

"For what?"

"For worrying more about what we thought than Colleen's feelings."

"Convince her to attend the party tonight, will you?" Robert asked.

"If you'll convince Jesse to come," Amelia challenged.

Robert's gaze swung to Jesse before returning to his sister. "Amelia—"

She climbed down the ladder, tossed a balled-up bit of silk at him, and continued on. "Help Jesse finish putting up the bows."

"Are you gonna talk her into coming?" he yelled after Amelia.

But she didn't answer before disappearing beyond the barn door. Robert scrambled up the ladder. "So are you going to come tonight?"

"Wasn't planning on it," Jesse answered, surprised the man had bothered to ask.

Robert clambered into the loft and made his way to a wall, where he dropped down and sighed heavily. "Women. I can't figure them out. Amelia is interested in you because she's not supposed to be. Colleen acts interested in me, but she tries to hide it. Makes no sense."

Jesse didn't particularly like hearing Robert's thinking on the reason that Amelia had shown an interest in him, but the words made sense. He'd been trying to figure it out for himself.

She had a passel of men to choose from. Men who'd never been to prison. Men who'd never broken the law. Men who at some point in their lives had probably been loved by someone.

Robert glared at him. "You think it makes sense?"

Jesse shrugged. "Maybe Colleen doesn't think she's good enough."

"That's crazy. Why would she think that?"

"I was just giving an opinion. It's been a while since I've spent much time with females, so my knowledge is a bit limited."

Robert snorted. "I don't think time spent with them makes a difference. How are your ribs?" he asked, changing the subject.

Jesse was really getting tired of everyone asking him that question, but still he answered. "Healing."

"That's good. Do you like Amelia?"

Jesse wondered if Robert was trying to trip him up by hopping back and forth between subjects.

"A man would be a fool not to, but I know my place, and I know it's not with her."

"You ever wish you hadn't robbed those banks?" Robert asked.

How was Jesse supposed to answer that? If he hadn't taken the money, he would have gone hungry, possibly died of starvation or cold or neglect. If he hadn't gotten caught, he never would have met Amelia. But was meeting her worth all the suffering he'd endured?

He slowly shook his head. "Can't say I do."

Robert grinned. "I'm beginning to think you're an honest outlaw. An outlaw by definition isn't honest, but somehow you are."

"I don't believe in lying or breaking my word," Jesse admitted.

"And Amelia?"

"Is better off if I stay away from her."

But he knew that was easier said than done.

CHAPTER SIXTEEN

Amelia found Colleen in her bedroom. Colleen's room was just down the hallway from Amelia's. Amelia had knocked on the door five times before Colleen had finally given her permission to enter.

Although Colleen was their servant, Amelia valued her friendship more than her skill at managing the house.

Colleen was sitting in a rocker, rocking fast and furiously, her arms folded against her stomach. "I'm not going to the dance, so save your breath," Colleen said.

Amelia sat on the edge of the bed. "Robert likes you."

"He likes to *kiss* me," Colleen admitted. "He's always sneaking into the kitchen when I'm baking to give me a little kiss. But you see how he reacts when he's caught. Indiscretion, indeed."

"I think he probably just said that because Jesse was there. He was worried about your reputation." Gnawing on her lower lip, Amelia scooted to the edge of the bed. "You must like kissing him. You didn't seem to try too hard to let him know Jesse and I were in the loft."

Colleen blushed and nodded. "I like kissing him."

"Then you'll enjoy dancing with him." Amelia dropped

to her knees in front of the rocker and took Colleen's hand. "Please go. You're my very best friend. I want you at my dance."

Colleen nodded. "All right. I'll go."

"And you'll dance with Robert?"

"If he asks."

Amelia hugged Colleen tightly. "Oh, he'll ask," she assured her.

She only hoped her brother had as much luck convincing Jesse to come.

"Look at that line of buggies," Colleen said.

Amelia joined her friend at the bedroom window and glanced out. As far as she could see, buggies were rolling along the dirt path that led from the main road to the ranch house. In addition to all the ranch hands, her father had invited various associates and important Fort Worth families. And, of course, their sons.

Tonight her father was at long last lifting his restriction. Tonight she could begin to be courted.

And he'd wanted her to have a host of eligible suitors from whom to choose. Unfortunately, she couldn't stop thinking about Jesse and hoping he'd be there.

"My goodness. I don't know how I'm going to remember everyone's name," Amelia said.

"You'll do just fine."

"From here, it sure looks like some of them are dressed

fancy. I think I actually see top hats."

"I've no doubt," Colleen said. "They'll be wanting to impress the judge's daughter."

Turning, Amelia took Colleen's hands. "Thank you for everything you've done to make tonight special."

Colleen had prepared a wonderful assortment of foods and arranged them on the large table in the dining room. Candles were flickering in crystal chandeliers in the parlor. Throughout the house flower arrangements sweetened each room.

"I was glad to do it for you," Colleen said, smiling.

"I'm so happy you'll be there."

"Somebody has to do the serving."

Amelia scowled at her. "The guests can serve themselves. Colleen, I want you to enjoy tonight. Maybe there's a gentleman for you."

"Why would I be wanting one?" she asked.

"To make Robert jealous?"

Colleen lowered her gaze. "He's a fine man, your brother is."

"Do you love him?"

"I don't know," Colleen admitted. "I know I can't sleep at night for thinking about him."

Amelia released Colleen's hands. "I feel the same way about Jesse."

"Amelia, he's an outlaw," Colleen reminded her.

"I know, but I want him to be here so badly, to dance

with him just once." She shook her head. "But I don't think he's going to come."

She gazed back out the window at the stream of buggies and carriages. Her father didn't even want her to be courted by one of the ranch hands. He preferred that a man of wealth and prestige set his sights on her.

She'd always anticipated this night with a great deal of enthusiasm.

And now she feared that no matter how wonderful it was, it would still leave her wanting. Still leave her longing for Jesse.

Jesse stood within the night shadows beneath a tree near the front porch. He hadn't planned to come to Amelia's party.

He'd been one of a half dozen ranch hands selected to show the arriving guests where to park their buggies. In his whole life, he'd never seen so many fancy-looking men.

He could tell that Mitch had been disappointed to see all these gentlemen arrive. Amelia certainly wasn't going to lack for suitors—or dance partners.

After Jesse had given oats to all the visiting horses, compliments of the judge, he'd gone to the bunkhouse and stretched out on his bed while the other men had gussied themselves up for tonight's event. He'd thought he might suffocate on the smell of all the hair oil they'd been using.

It wasn't until after they'd left that he'd decided he

wanted to take a bath. That had led to his shaving, trimming his hair, and putting on the white shirt he'd stored in the small trunk beside his bunk after the trip to Fort Worth with Amelia.

He'd decided that since he was spruced up, he might as well just mosey on over. Now he stood there, trying to gather his courage to step inside.

Light spilled out through the windows. He heard a cacophony of sounds: laughter, voices, music.

The door was open, inviting folks in. Every now and then he'd see people pass through the entryway. But he had yet to see Amelia. It was her special night. With so many guests, he doubted he'd be noticed.

All he wanted was to catch a glimpse of her.

Shoving his hands into his trouser pockets, he walked into the house. He felt self-conscious, but he was also enthralled. Jovial voices and laughter echoed around him.

In the judge's library, men smoked cigars. He'd never seen as much food and drink in one place as he did in the dining room, where people stood around holding plates and eating while they talked.

He thought the men far outnumbered the women. His suspicions were confirmed when he wended his way through the crowds and finally entered the parlor. Young men lined the walls, while those fortunate enough to have claimed a woman were dancing to the music provided by several older men with violins.

Candles flickered in the gilded chandeliers, illuminating those who waltzed in the center of the room.

Jesse's gaze was immediately drawn to Amelia—as though no one else existed. He'd always thought she was pretty. Tonight she was stunning.

Her hair was piled on top of her head. Curling tendrils bounced along the nape of her neck. Her green dress revealed her alabaster throat and shoulders.

But her appeal went beyond her clothes. Her eyes sparkled like emeralds held up to the sun. Her smile dazzled with its brilliance.

Her obvious joy radiated around her—around her and her partner.

She was dancing with Mitch Monroe.

Amelia was having the time of her life—and yet she felt as though something were missing. No matter with whom she danced, her gaze kept darting beyond her partner to take in the men standing along the walls, to see who was there—and who wasn't.

She'd never before danced continuously; she'd never before had constant attention paid to her. She knew she should have been warmed by the flattery that each gentleman bestowed upon her.

But no one was truly able to hold her attention. No one made her heart kick up into an excited beat. No one made her palms grow damp. No one made her ache with longing when he kissed her hand before passing her on to the next fellow for a dance.

Every now and then her gaze would fall on Robert and Colleen. He'd obviously convinced her to dance with him, and just as obviously he wasn't willing to allow anyone else a turn—if anyone had been foolish enough to ask.

It was so incredibly apparent watching them that they had eyes only for each other. Their gazes were locked. Neither was distracted like Amelia was—always looking for something more.

She envied them their contentment with each other. She wished she could feel satisfied with the evening. She knew she had no reason to be disappointed. The night was wonderful, the gentlemen were charming and handsome, and her father was beaming with pride.

But then she caught sight of the reason for her discontent. For the span of a heartbeat, she saw Jesse in the crowd. Her heart kicked up its tempo as it rejoiced because he'd come after all.

And just as quickly he disappeared, and she couldn't have been more disappointed.

"Amelia, did you hear what I said?"

She returned her attention to Mitch. "What?"

He laughed lightly. "I was wondering if you might like to take a walk with me outside."

A walk sounded wonderful. More time spent with Mitch, however, didn't. And she couldn't explain why. He'd been working for her father for three years now. She'd always enjoyed his company, knew he had an interest in her. He was handsome, fun.

She also understood that he wanted more than a walk. He wanted to take her somewhere private for a kiss. She could see the desire reflected in his eyes. And she simply wasn't interested.

"I'm sorry, Mitch, but I promised Mr. Thomaston the next dance." Although she suspected the young banker would be willing to step aside.

The music drifted into silence.

"Perhaps later," he said, then kissed the back of her hand.

True to her word, she danced with the banker, and then she waltzed with her father.

"Are you enjoying yourself?" he asked.

She smiled brightly. "Of course. Aren't you?"

"Not really. It's difficult to watch all these men showing such a keen interest in my daughter," he admitted. "Makes me realize that before long I'll be losing you."

"Oh, Papa, you'll never lose me. I'll always be your little girl."

"Perhaps. But you'll be some man's wife, some child's mother. Choose wisely, Amelia," he cautioned.

"I'm not in any hurry, Papa. As a matter of fact, I'm contemplating attending a university." She took a deep breath and confessed, "I think I'd like to become a lawyer."

He gave her a speculative look. "Anyone in particular you're looking to defend?"

She laughed. "It's a little late to defend Jesse, if that's what you're thinking. But the more I get to know him, the more he seems like an unlikely person to be an outlaw."

"He admitted it, Amelia. For whatever reason, he stole."

"I'm not saying what he did was right. I just think things are a bit more complicated than we realize. And if you didn't feel the same way, you wouldn't have given him this chance to finish out his sentence here."

He grinned. "Maybe you *should* study the law. You always did like to argue."

The music came to an end, as did the dance with her father.

Then there was Robert. "I'd like a dance with my sister," he said.

When the music began again and they were dancing, Amelia said, "I'm surprised you'd give up a dance with Colleen."

"David wanted one dance with her, and I wanted to thank you for convincing her to come."

She smiled. "You like her a lot, don't you?"

He nodded. "More than a lot, actually. She's given me permission to court her."

"Oh, Robert, that's wonderful!"

"I'm pretty happy about it, and I intend to see that she's

happy, too. I'm sorry I couldn't talk Jesse into coming."

But he had been here, for only a moment.

"I don't know what to make of the outlaw," Robert said quietly. "He broke the law, but he seems like a decent enough fella. I actually think under different circumstances he and I could have been friends."

Amelia couldn't help but wonder if under different circumstances she and Jesse could have been sweethearts.

The music drifted into silence.

"I need to get back to Colleen," Robert said.

Amelia watched him walk away. She was so incredibly happy for her brother and Colleen.

A gentleman quickly approached. Amelia smiled at him and shook her head. "I think I'm going to sit this one out."

"Would you like me to get you something to drink?" he asked eagerly.

"Thank you, but I'm going to step outside for some air."

CHAPTER SEVENTEEN

On the back porch, Amelia looked out on the night. A full moon sent its silver beams over the landscape. A warm breeze toyed with her hair.

She took a deep breath and smelled the honeysuckle her mother had planted years ago. At special moments like this, she missed her most of all.

It seemed as though she'd waited her whole life for this one night, this moment when she was allowed to step over the threshold into womanhood. She'd anticipated its arrival, and although it was far grander than she'd imagined it would be . . . it still left her wanting something more.

She saw a movement out of the corner of her eye. Turning slightly, she spotted Jesse leaning against the house, a silhouette outlined by shadows, his white shirt in stark contrast to the night.

She stepped off the porch and walked over to him, voicing what she knew she wanted more than anything else. "Come inside and dance with me."

"You don't want to be seen dancing with an outlaw, Amelia," he said quietly.

"Maybe not, but I wouldn't mind being seen dancing with Jesse Lawton. I saw you inside earlier. Why didn't you stay?"

"Because it hurts."

Concern furrowed her brow. "Your ribs are aching?"

"No. It hurts to see all the things I've never had, everything I'll never have."

"You could have it all, Jesse. As soon as you've finished serving your time, you can do anything, be anything you want," she said earnestly.

"You really believe that, don't you?" he asked quietly.

"With all my heart. You robbed a few banks. You shouldn't have done it, but you never hurt anyone. Papa believes there's good in you, or he wouldn't be giving you this chance. And I *know* there is or I wouldn't be standing here with you now."

"You've got a passel of men inside the house wanting to court you."

"I know, and not one measures up to you."

"Amelia, you don't even know me."

Taking his roughened hand, she threaded her fingers through his. "I know you're gentle with animals. They're not easily fooled, Jesse. But they trust you.

"I know you've had a hard life. It doesn't sound like anyone ever treated you fairly. Maybe you got lost for a while, but with a little guidance it seems to me that you could travel a road that would take you to grand dreams.

"You've run away from so many people in your life, Jesse. I think you could run from here and my brothers wouldn't find you. No matter how good they are at tracking. You're better at running."

She lifted her gaze to his. The darkness didn't prevent her from seeing the blue in his eyes. The color was written on her heart. "Don't run from me," she pleaded softly.

"You don't know what you're asking, Amelia," he rasped.

"So many people have hurt you, Jesse. Trust me not to."

"But what if *I* hurt *you*? My past—"

"Is your past. Let it go."

Music drifted out of the house, soft and low, lyrical and sweet. "Dance with me."

"I can't. Not inside," he said quietly.

"Then dance with me here."

"Amelia, I've never danced," he said. "I watched the couples inside, but I don't know if I can do it."

Her heart ached at the shame that she heard reflected in his low voice.

"It's not that hard, Jesse."

Sensing his hesitation, she tightened her hold on his fingers and placed her other hand on his shoulder.

"Put your free hand on my waist," she told him.

When he did, she said, "Simply step back and I'll follow."

His steps were awkward, slow, hesitant, not the movements of a true waltz, not taken in beat to the music. But she didn't care.

At long last, she was experiencing what she'd expected to feel all night: anticipation, a thrill, absolute joy.

She had danced with bankers, lawyers, businessmen, cattle owners, and cowhands. She'd danced with wealthy gentlemen and men whose greatest gift to her would be their hearts.

Yet none of them touched her as Jesse did. None made her soul sing, her heart pound, or her body tingle.

What was it about him that drew her in? His soulful eyes? His tragic past? His undetermined future?

She couldn't really say. She knew only that when she was with him, she felt as though she was truly becoming the woman she'd always imagined she could be.

In time Jesse began to move with a poetic rhythm, holding her close as though she were as precious as handblown glass. In the faint moonlight, she could see that his gaze never wandered from hers. It was as though they were alone in the world, and at this moment, she had no desire to be anyplace else.

The music wafted into silence, but she still heard the strains echoing around her as she and Jesse ceased to waltz.

He bent his head and touched his mouth to hers.

Within his kiss she sensed all the loneliness he'd held at bay, all the hurt that haunted him, all the love he dared not hope to find. He poured himself into the kiss, and she could do no less.

Rising up on her toes, she wrapped her arms around his neck and returned the kiss with equal yearning for all that might be: for dreams promised, but as yet unfulfilled.

For all they might share if only they were both willing to take the risk.

Walking toward the bunkhouse, Jesse realized that for the first time in his life he felt like whistling a joyous tune. Amelia believed in him. Believed in his goodness. Thought he was worthy of her affections.

He was sure of her feelings. The warm way she'd looked at him while they'd danced. The manner in which she'd melted into that kiss.

When she'd spotted him beneath the tree watching her, she could simply have gone back into the house. Instead she'd approached him.

She made him think that he could do anything he wanted. He could raise horses, as he'd often dreamed. Breed them, train them, and sell them. Make a decent living.

But more than that, she made him believe that maybe he could acquire all the things that so many folks took for granted. A house that carried the scent of a woman, that rang with laughter. A place where people could feel good about each other and not hurt each other.

A place where maybe other boys without parents could come and work. Jesse would never beat them or make them feel worthless. He'd praise them for their efforts and encourage them as he'd never been encouraged. The way he saw Tanner telling the men when they did a good job.

He'd never realized how important words were. More often than not, the back of a hand had told him when he was doing wrong. Or the booming voice of a judge in a courtroom.

Amelia was right. He could travel down a different road and give himself a life he could be proud of. And maybe, eventually, he could share that life with her.

He almost laughed out loud. He was getting way ahead of himself here. First he had to finish out his time, and then he could see about pursuing some of his dreams.

But until he'd met Amelia, he'd never contemplated truly following them.

He neared the bunkhouse. Not a glimmer of light escaped from the windows. He figured most of the men were still at the house, vying for Amelia's attention. He practically wanted to shout with the joy bubbling up inside him. He'd never in his life been this happy.

As though anything was possible. All things were achievable.

From out of the shadows someone lunged toward him. Before he could react, a hand clamped over his mouth and an arm wrapped around his chest, pinning him against a hard body that was dragging him deeper into the night.

He tried to buck free.

"Stop fighting me, boy!" a harsh voice demanded.

Recognizing the voice, he did as instructed. But his heart pounded unmercifully and the blood thrummed between his temples, making him dizzy.

It couldn't be. It absolutely couldn't be.

The man removed his hand from Jesse's mouth and quickly spun him around. Jesse could barely see the face clearly in the shadows, but he didn't need to. He recognized the scent of whiskey and stale cigar smoke.

"Pete, what are you doing here?" Jesse asked.

He saw the familiar grin take shape in the distant moonlight. Pete was a big man with a thick neck that had saved him from the hangman's noose.

"Heard you was out of prison," Pete said in a voice that sounded as though he still had a rope pressed against his throat. "Just wanted to see for myself."

"How'd you hear that?" Jesse asked.

"Me and the boys was passin' through Fort Worth.

Stopped in a saloon. You know how I enjoy a good saloon and an interestin' poker game."

Jesse nodded. "Yeah. I remember."

"Well, now, I was playin' with a couple of fellas this evening. One kept exercisin' his jaws, tellin' us about this big celebration that a judge was puttin' on for his girl. Judge Harper.

"Then the fella went on to say how the judge had made arrangements to have an outlaw serve out his time at his ranch. Dang it, boy, my glass eye 'bout popped out of its socket when he said your name. And I knew I had to come see you."

"I'm glad you did, Pete, but I'm not sure it's wise for you to be seen around here."

Pete chuckled low. "You ain't changed much, have you, Jesse? Still worryin' 'bout ol' Pete."

"It's just that the judge has all these rules—"

"Rules don't bother me, boy. They never have. I figure they were made to be broken."

"Yeah, but—"

"No buts about it. Now, I want you to listen careful, 'cause I got us a plan."

Jesse's stomach started to tighten. Pete's last plan had landed him in prison.

"Pete—"

"Shh, Jesse. I need you to listen now. My hearin' ain't what it used to be. I've lost my talent for opening safes, so me and the boys have had to turn to other means to make our money."

"You mean that you've gone honest?"

"Heck fire, no!"

Jesse could hear the undercurrent of laughter in Pete's voice.

Pete leaned near, bringing his unpleasant breath with him. Funny how it had never really bothered Jesse until now, how he was looking at Pete through a different set of eyes. Looking at him as he imagined Amelia would.

She'd be disgusted by what she saw.

"We've taken to robbin' passengers on trains. But we don't make much, and we gotta take from a lot of folks to make the effort worth our while. But I'm sittin' at that card table tonight listenin' to that fella talkin' 'bout how successful Harper is with his judgeship and his ranch and his cattle. And I'm thinkin' it ain't fair. He needs to spread the wealth a bit. But how am I gonna get him to do that?

"And then it hits me. His daughter."

The hairs on the back of Jesse's neck bristled. "Amelia?"

"Yep. I just figured I'd take the little lady, and the judge could pay me a bundle of money to get her back unharmed."

A fissure of fear ripped through Jesse. "Pete, no disrespect, but I don't think that plan is going to work."

"Had doubts myself about it workin' 'till I seen you kiss the judge's daughter."

Jesse's stomach quivered with the thought that Pete had been spying on them.

"You were watching us?"

"Watchin', listenin', workin' up a plan better than the one I had before. And here it is: you lure the judge's daughter out of the house and we take her."

"No!" Jesse took a step back and repeated, "No. I'm not going to help you kidnap Amelia."

Pete knotted Jesse's shirt in his beefy fist and tugged him closer.

"Yes, you will. I want that man's money."

Pete released his hold and pushed Jesse back.

Jesse slid his eyes closed. Maybe when he opened them, he'd discover that he'd been asleep and all this was just a nightmare. But when he opened them, Pete's silhouette was still there to haunt him.

"Think about it, Jesse," Pete said in a conspiratorial voice. "Do you honestly think the folks around here are gonna believe you had nothin' to do with us takin' her?"

Jesse thought about how quickly they'd jumped him when Amelia's horse had thrown her. They'd think the worst.

"You're gonna be blamed," Pete said with conviction. "You might as well help us out and share in the reward."

Jesse released a deep sigh, stalling for time while he

tried to figure a way out. He could agree to help them, and then warn Judge Harper. He didn't know if the man would believe him, but he knew that Amelia would. "All right. Pete, I'll help you."

Pete clapped his hand on Jesse's shoulder. "Good boy. And don't get any ideas about warnin' anyone. You don't fulfill your end of the bargain and that sweet little lady is likely to get hurt real bad."

Jesse clenched his fists at his sides to keep them from hitting Pete in the mouth. He'd never known such anger or frustration.

"I said I'd help you. I didn't say I'd kidnap Amelia. I've got a better plan. I've seen the judge's safe. He keeps it in his office in the house. If all you want is his money, I can get it for you."

He'd never planned to steal again, but he didn't see that he had much choice. If Pete was determined to get the judge's money one way or another, Jesse could hand it over to him without involving Amelia.

Of course, afterward he'd be on the run—or back in prison. Pete was right about everyone thinking the worst of him. When the money was discovered missing, they'd all be pointing the finger at him. As soon as he walked out of the judge's house with the loot, he'd have to keep walking.

"He keeps his money in the house?" Pete asked.

"Why else would he have a safe?"

"Well, well, well," Pete muttered. "Who would have thought they'd be dumb enough to put the fox in the henhouse?"

Jesse knew Pete was considering him to be the fox.

"So we'll just take the money and leave the girl?"

"Yeah. There's less risk of us gettin' caught this way, too. You was always a smart thinker, Jesse. But there's too many folks around right now. Tomorrow night, though—"

"No. I've gotta do it tonight, Pete. By tomorrow I might chicken out. When the guests leave, I'll give the judge's family time to fall asleep. Then I'll slip into the house and get the money. There's a shack on the north end of the ranch. You just ride straight north from here. You'll see a windmill. It's near there. I'll meet you at the shack just before dawn with the money."

"I don't know, boy. I'm thinkin' I need to go into the house with you. Be there when you open the safe—just in case you have a change of heart at the last minute, like you did durin' our last robbery."

"I won't change my mind." He'd do anything to keep Amelia safe.

"But remember, if you don't uphold your end of the bargain, don't meet me at dawn, that little lady might end up gettin' hurt real bad."

"I'll keep my end. You just leave her alone."

Pete cackled. "I was right. You do care for her. She'll

be fine as long as you put the money in my hand. I'll see you at dawn, then. It's good to be workin' with you again."

Pete quickly disappeared into the darkness.

With his body quaking so badly that he was surprised he remained upright, Jesse turned and headed toward the bunkhouse.

He wanted to run like he'd never run before.

Amelia was wrong. He couldn't escape his past. It would always catch up with him.

CHAPTER EIGHTEEN

Lying in bed, Amelia couldn't stop thinking about Jesse.

After he'd kissed her, she'd gone back into the house and danced with other gentlemen. She'd been polite and shown interest in their conversations. She'd smiled, laughed, and flirted.

But it had all seemed meaningless.

No one fascinated her as Jesse did. No one set her heart to beating faster.

She thought she was quite possibly falling in love with him.

Never having been in love before, she couldn't be certain if what she was feeling was indeed love. But it simply made sense to her that it had to be.

Why else would she think about him constantly?

Click.

Her breath caught at the unexpected sound.

Clink.

She moved nothing but her eyes as she searched the room trying to determine where the noise had come from.

Clack.

The window.

She scrambled out of bed and rushed to the window. She could see the silhouette of a familiar figure standing in the moonlight. Another tiny rock hit the glass.

She raised the window and leaned out. "Jesse?"

"Get dressed to ride and come down here," he whispered in a voice loud enough for her to hear.

Dressed to ride? That made no sense. It was the middle of the night.

"What are you talking about?"

"We're going after the white mustang," he called up.

"Now?"

"Now," he answered.

Goodness gracious!

"I'll be right down!"

She couldn't believe it as she tore off her nightgown and hurried to change into her split riding skirt. She stilled.

She couldn't do this. Yes, she was finally seventeen. She was allowed to have gentlemen callers, but she still wasn't allowed to spend time alone with Jesse. Dancing with him outside—alone—had been unexpected, and they'd been fortunate that no one had spotted them.

But she couldn't deliberately go with him now, because she knew that in so doing, she risked having him sent back to prison.

Still, she finished dressing. She decided that explaining

the situation to him in person would be better than yelling out the window and hoping no one heard them.

Opening the door, she glanced cautiously into the darkened hallway. No one was about. She imagined everyone was sleeping soundly after dancing most of the night.

She crept down the stairs and made her way outside. Jesse stood in the shadows beside the front porch. He already had two horses saddled and waiting. The temptation to go with him was almost more than she could bear.

She crossed the porch and wrapped her arms around a beam to keep from advancing farther. "Jesse, we can't do this."

"Yes, we can."

She shook her head. "I told you what my father said. If he finds out that I went off with you alone, he'll send you back to prison."

"I know." He bent his head. "During my whole life, Amelia, I've never given anyone a gift." He lifted his gaze to hers. "I want to capture this horse for you."

"In the morning when Papa wakes up, we'll get permission—"

"It has to be now."

"Why? Why can't we wait?" she asked, confused by his insistence that they go right now.

"Trust me, Amelia. Please."

During the time he'd been here, Jesse had never asked

anything of her. Never asked anything of anyone that she knew of.

"But you're risking—"

"I know what I'm risking. I'm going after that horse one way or another. I'd rather you go with me."

"I didn't think you wanted to capture the mustang," she reminded him.

"I changed my mind," he said before turning away from her and mounting a horse.

"Why?" she asked.

"It's your birthday, and I want to give you something special, something no one else can." He prodded his horse into a gentle lope.

She waited a heartbeat before climbing onto Duchess and following him.

As he galloped his horse over the moon-washed landscape, Jesse was relieved that Amelia was riding beside him. He knew a chance existed that they wouldn't find the horse before anyone noticed they were gone.

But he also knew that horses tended to range in the same place. Amelia knew where the mustang she was interested in grazed, and with luck, they'd find it.

Earlier he'd lain in his bed and listened while the men had returned from the party long after he had, guffawing and making a ruckus as though they didn't have a worry in the world.

While he'd been contemplating his fate and his options.

If he told anyone about Pete—and Pete found out—Amelia would pay the price for his betrayal. Jesse knew Pete well enough to know that he never made empty threats. Oddly, it was one of the first things that Jesse had admired about the man. He kept his promises, even when they involved retribution.

Jesse realized now—a little too late—that he'd been a stupid kid at twelve when he'd grabbed onto Pete's shirttail.

If he did as Pete demanded, no one would get hurt. But Jesse would have to run. He figured he might even succeed at escaping. If he didn't, he'd go back to prison. Either way, he'd never see Amelia again.

That thought caused an unbearable ache in his chest.

So he'd decided to capture one last memory with her—and grant her wish in the process.

He just didn't see any other way out of his dilemma.

And he wanted—needed—these last few hours with Amelia. To pretend for a little while, at least, that he was like every other fella she'd danced with . . . to imagine that his past was untainted and he was good enough for her.

Even though he now understood that he never would be. He'd always be shackled to his past.

He slowed his horse as they neared the rise where they'd been going that fateful day when she'd fallen from her horse and he'd taken the beating. She drew up alongside him.

"Why couldn't we wait to go after the mustang?" she asked.

It was the first opportunity they'd had to speak to each other since they'd headed out. He'd purposefully kept them traveling at a rapid pace, hoping she'd forget his words. Apparently she'd been chewing on them since he'd spoken them.

He glanced over at her. She was beautiful, limned by the moonlight. He knew he'd never forget Amelia's delicate features. She was emblazoned on his heart.

Where had that poetic notion come from? Before her, his life certainly hadn't allowed for such fanciful thoughts. And in another day or so, they'd once again become foreign.

"I just figured you wouldn't have much time for me once all those fellas you were dancing with tonight start calling on you," he lied.

He couldn't tell her the truth because her dedication to justice would require she tell her father—even if it meant putting herself at risk. He hoped she did become a lawyer someday. Maybe if he'd had someone like her, someone he could have trusted, he might not have found himself punished so harshly at such an early age.

She laughed softly. "It's not like a gentleman will take me away from the ranch and hold me prisoner while he's courting me."

He could only hope no one would abduct her. He tried to make light of his earlier comment. "You'll have to forgive me, but I don't have experience when it comes to wooing."

"It makes me sad when I think of all the things you've missed out on, Jesse."

"I don't want to make you sad. I just want to get the horse for you." So she'd have something to remember him by. He wouldn't be around long enough to gentle it, but hopefully someone else would.

They brought their horses to the top of the rise. He heard Amelia catch her breath. His very nearly stopped.

Beneath the vast expanse of stars, a herd of mustangs rested. At the edge of the group, pacing like a sentry, was a white horse. Jesse had no doubt this animal was a stallion, setting itself up to guard the herd.

"Isn't he beautiful?" Amelia whispered.

"That must be his bunch of mares," Jesse said, his voice equally low. "Probably his foals as well."

"I hadn't considered that he'd have offspring," she mused.

He imagined there were a lot of things that a person who'd always had freedom didn't take into consideration.

"I have to figure out the best way to capture him," he told her. "Why don't we stretch out here on the rise and watch them while I figure out a plan?"

Amelia lay on the ground, her hand wrapped around Jesse's. He'd stiffened when she'd first taken it. She didn't think he was accustomed to being touched. It had taken him a few minutes to finally relax.

His hand was rougher than hers. Calluses lined the pads of his palm and the tips of his fingers. But she felt the strength he possessed, even at rest.

She was torn between watching him and focusing her attention on the mustangs. Jesse had told her that as long as they stayed upwind of the herd, they probably wouldn't be detected. He'd tethered their horses on the other side of the rise, away from the herd.

"Does he ever sleep?" she asked quietly as the white stallion continued to amble back and forth.

"I imagine. When I make my move, the horses will take off at a gallop. The fastest mare will lead them. She's his favorite," he told her.

"How do you know?" she asked.

"I've spent a lot of time under the stars, a lot of time watching horses. The stallion always favors the fastest and the smartest. She'll be the one in the front."

"I figured he'd lead them," she admitted.

"No. He's probably the quickest of all, but he'll run at the rear, putting himself between the herd and us. Even though it increases his risk of capture, he'll hang back. He'll sacrifice himself to protect his mares."

She turned her head so she could look at him. He was already watching her, and she wondered how long his gaze had been focused on her.

"What will the mares do once you capture their leader?" she asked, suddenly worried about their survival.

"There's probably a younger stallion in the group who's been biding his time, waiting to challenge the lead stallion. He'll take over, or maybe a couple of stallions will battle it out to determine who is in charge."

She returned her attention to the herd. She could see foals nestled close to their mothers. "Do you really think those are his colts and fillies?"

"He wouldn't let another horse mate with his mares."

"It seems sort of sad to take him away from them," she said softly.

"Yeah, it does."

She watched the animals for several minutes before daring to ask, "But you'll do it?"

He rose up on his elbow, drawing himself closer to her until she could no longer see the stars, until all she could see was the shadow of his face.

"If that's what you want," he said quietly.

"But you don't want to do it, do you?" she asked.

"I'll do it for you."

She trailed her fingers along his cheek. What sort of man was he? He cared so much about the freedom of a wild horse . . . and yet he had no regard for the law.

"Why did you rob the banks?"

Against her palm, she felt his throat work as he swallowed.

"Because I was hungry, scared. I'd done without for so long that when Pete said that money was just sitting there not being used, I believed him. When we discovered that I was skilled at opening a safe, I felt important. I was tired of feeling like something to be scraped off somebody's boot. In the end, though, I felt lower than a snail's belly."

"You mean when you got caught?"

He shook his head. "After we robbed the first bank. When we made camp that night and Pete counted out the money and tossed my share over to me, it just didn't feel right resting in my hand. When we stopped in a little town, I took what I needed from my stash for supplies and left the rest in a church."

Stunned, she asked, "You gave most of it away?"

"Yeah. Pretty dumb, huh?"

She didn't think it was dumb at all.

"Did you tell them what you did with the money during your trial?"

He shrugged. "Nobody asked. Besides, what I did with the money wasn't important. What mattered was that I'd robbed the bank to begin with."

But she couldn't help but believe that a judge might not have been so harsh with his sentence if he'd known how Jesse had disbursed his share of the money.

"Did you do that after every bank robbery?"

"No," he admitted.

Her heart sank. Every time she saw good, he snatched it away.

"So you started keeping it," she said.

"No. I just didn't always give it to the church. Some towns don't have a church. So I'd leave it at the school or on someone's doorstep. I didn't like it burning a hole in my pocket."

She cradled his cheek. "Jesse, that's admirable . . . in an odd sort of way."

"Amelia, I still robbed the banks."

"Why? After the first one, after you realized you weren't going to keep the money, why did you continue to steal?" she asked.

"Because I liked riding with the Nightriders. I was twelve when I first hooked up with them. For two years no one beat me or yelled at me or called me worthless. For the first time in my life, I felt as though I belonged. I didn't want to lose that."

He wasn't exactly Robin Hood. And yet something about his actions seemed commendable in a strange sort of way. No doubt she was simply looking at him with her heart rather than her common sense.

Since he seemed willing to talk about his past in ways he hadn't before, she decided to take the conversation a step farther.

"Jesse, I was wondering . . . during that last bank robbery, how is it that you were the only member of the gang to get caught?"

"I didn't leave when Pete told me to."

She tried to recall what she knew about the bank robbery. "I remember reading that it happened at night. I know Pete shot a clerk. But what was the clerk doing there?"

"Working, I reckon. He came out of a back office. Guess he heard us making a commotion, so he decided to investigate. He surprised us. And Pete doesn't like surprises. He fired his gun without thinking."

"But the clerk didn't die, did he?" she asked.

"Nope. He lived to tell the marshal that Pete had shot him."

"You sound almost bitter that he did," she said. "If he hadn't told the authorities who shot him, they might have thought *you'd* done it!"

"I don't resent what he told them," he told her. "I begrudge what he *didn't* tell them."

"And what was that?" she prodded.

"It doesn't matter now. It was a long time ago."

But it did matter. To her. A man had been shot, almost killed. Jesse had been there. It could have so easily been him who wounded the clerk.

Reaching out, she cradled his cheek. She wanted to believe in Jesse, but it was difficult with this wall standing between them. "Please tell me what you wanted him to say."

He shook his head. "I was such a fool. Young, naive.

I wanted him . . . thought he would put in a good word for me."

She furrowed her brow. "Jesse, the Nightriders broke into the bank and shot him! I imagine he felt that at least one of you going to prison was owed to him for what he'd suffered."

"But he owed *me!*"

She stared through the night at him, wishing she had a lantern so she could see into his eyes more clearly. "Why in the world do you think he owed you anything?"

"Because I stayed behind. I stayed behind and kept my hands pressed to his wound so the blood wouldn't flow so fast. I stayed behind knowing I'd get caught!"

Her heart thundering, she sat up. She didn't know how to respond. Her father had never mentioned this aspect of the case. She wondered if he knew. But how could anyone know if the clerk had never told?

"You stayed behind on purpose?" she asked softly. "I mean, you had a chance to escape?"

"Pete and the others got away. Pete tried to get me to go with him. He grabbed my arm, but I jerked free. There was so much blood. I was afraid the clerk would bleed to death if no one stayed to help him. Pete told me that I'd be on my own.

"Somebody must have heard the gunshot," Jesse continued. "It didn't take long for the law to arrive. The clerk probably would have been all right if I hadn't stayed."

He shook his head slowly. "I foolishly thought if I helped the fella that he'd explain what I'd done, and that it would make a difference to somebody." He shrugged. "But he didn't."

Before tonight she'd never really wondered how it was that he was the only member of the gang to have been captured. She'd expected him to say that he'd been wounded, left behind for dead. Abandoned.

In a way he had been, but it had been his choice.

"Didn't you tell the authorities why you'd stayed behind?"

"No one was interested in what a fourteen-year-old kid had to say."

She was horrified at the thought. "But at your trial—"

"They put the clerk on the stand. He told them that we broke into the bank, and Pete shot him. What he told them was true. He just didn't tell them everything."

Jesse was a contradiction, inherently good, convinced to do bad. If she'd been his lawyer, she would have played on that aspect of his life. She would have presented the whole story to the jury and the judge.

"So no one ever knew you might have saved the man's life," she mused. "We should tell my father."

"Amelia, it doesn't matter anymore. The past is the past. I don't want to think about it, and I don't want to talk about it. I've got to get you back to the house long before dawn, so I need to get busy capturing that stallion for you."

He started to get up. She wrapped her hand around his arm. He stilled.

"There's goodness in you, Jesse Lawton. I want my father to know about it."

"It won't make any difference."

She couldn't blame him for not believing that it would. Pete had rewarded him with kind words when he'd done bad things. No one had ever praised him or shown him appreciation when he'd deserved it.

"I don't want you to capture the stallion," she said quietly.

In the waning moonlight, she saw him smile . . . the most beautiful smile he'd ever bestowed upon her.

It took her breath away.

She knew, deep within her heart, that he'd brought her here hoping she'd abandon her quest for the stallion. His gift to her had become a night beneath the stars, a night of awakening, a time of sharing like he'd never given her before.

"Remember this night, Amelia. No matter what happens, remember this night."

He lowered his mouth to hers and kissed her tenderly.

Remember this night? How could she ever forget it? For them, it was the start of a new beginning.

Jesse drew away from her, took her hand, got to his feet, and pulled her up to hers.

"I need to get you home," he said.

"What did you mean by 'no matter what happens'?" she asked.

"I know I can't keep seeing you like this. Sooner or later somebody will find out. I don't expect you to wait five years for another dance."

He led her to her horse and helped her into the saddle. Gazing down at him, she didn't think she'd have to wait five years. Not once she told her father everything Jesse had revealed tonight.

CHAPTER NINETEEN

Standing within the night shadows of the barn, Jesse watched the house. He'd escorted Amelia to her front door, given her one last, lingering kiss, and left her with the lie that he'd see to the horses.

He'd unsaddled Duchess. But the horse he'd ridden to the rise earlier remained saddled. He'd located a worn but empty saddlebag in the tack room.

After tonight he'd be unable to turn back. Jesse would be an outlaw for the rest of his life.

He'd lose whatever affection Amelia had for him.

He'd be on the run.

But she'd be safe.

That was all that mattered to him.

Jesse had been waiting for lamplight to appear in Amelia's window. Long minutes had passed. It suddenly occurred to him that she might slip into her room and get ready for bed in the dark. She wouldn't want to chance waking someone up.

He glanced at the far horizon. It wouldn't be much longer before the sun began to appear. If he was going to break into the safe, he needed to do it now.

He took a deep breath to steel his resolve. He didn't much like that he was betraying the judge and Amelia and everyone else at the ranch who had treated him decently since the day of misunderstanding.

But he didn't see that he had much choice.

He glanced around. No movement. The men weren't stirring yet, but soon they would be. Leading the horse behind him and loathing each stride that took him closer, he walked to the house. The moon was a silver orb that guided him.

He tethered the horse to a nearby bush. He crept across the porch and placed his hand on the doorknob. He turned it.

Locked.

He took a slender piece of wire out of his pocket and hunkered in front of the door. In the beginning Pete had used him to climb to the roof and slip inside because he was small and skinny.

But in time, as he'd begun to fill out, he'd had to find another way to help Pete get inside buildings. So he'd learned how to pick locks. He wasn't particularly proud of the skill, so he'd decided not to tell Amelia that he had the ability to—

Click!

—open a locked door with nothing more than wire and patience.

He stuck his head through the opened door and glanced around. All was still. All was quiet.

He moved stealthily to the judge's library. He could see the silhouette of a chair and the desk. He walked cautiously to the desk and found the lamp.

He struck a match, lit the lamp, and turned the flame down low. He carried the lamp to the safe and set it on the floor.

He knelt beside the safe, pressed his ear to the cool metal, and turned the dial. His heart was pounding so loudly that he could barely hear the motion of the tumblers.

Concentrate, he commanded himself.

His palms grew damp. He wiped them on his britches. Britches the judge had provided.

Gritting his teeth, he focused all his efforts on the safe. The slow, careful turning of the knob.

Clink.

A tumbler fell.

He rotated the dial the other way.

Clank.

Another tumbler.

He turned the knob.

Click.

He jerked the handle down and swung open the door. The paper money was arranged in five neat stacks. A pouch rested in front. He snatched up the pouch and heard the clink of coins.

He didn't bother to check the coins or count the currency as he stuffed it all into the saddlebag. Pete could worry about the particulars later. He only hoped there was enough here to satisfy Pete's greed.

Strange how he'd always thought rich folks were greedy because they possessed money. But the Harpers had given him an abundance of things, including a second chance.

"What are you doing?"

He twisted around. Amelia stood in the doorway.

He felt as though someone had thrust a rusty bayonet into his chest.

He surged to his feet and quickly crossed the room, intending simply to edge past her.

She grabbed his arm. "Jesse?"

"If you care for me at all, give me a two-hour head start before you tell anyone what I've done."

She shook her head. "I don't understand. Why are you doing this?"

He jerked free of her hold, revealing the truth that he wished was a lie. "Once an outlaw, always an outlaw."

He strode out of the house, holding his breath, expecting to hear her yell for her father.

But only silence followed in his wake.

He mounted the horse, brought it about, and glanced back over his shoulder. She stood in the doorway, watching him.

He urged the horse into a gallop, knowing he would forever see the devastation of his betrayal reflected in Amelia Harper's eyes.

Amelia sat in the chair in her father's library, watching as he and her brothers loaded their rifles.

Jesse had asked her to give him two hours.

She'd given him a full two minutes.

After they'd returned from their excursion to search for the mustang, she'd gone to the parlor where she'd danced with so many gentlemen during her party. She'd thought about them, thought about Jesse.

She'd come to the conclusion that she did indeed love Jesse Lawton. She'd been on her way to her bedroom when she'd spotted the low light coming out of the library. She'd assumed she'd find her father at his desk reading his law books and contemplating some aspect of a trial.

She'd wanted to share her revelation with him, tell him all she'd learned about Jesse, and determine whether she had enough information for him to reconsider Jesse's sentence.

Instead she'd discovered Jesse taking the money that her father kept in the safe so he could pay the men each month. He kept the bulk of his wealth in a bank in Fort Worth. So what Jesse had taken, her father could afford to lose.

But it was the principle of the thing. She knew her father felt as though he'd been stabbed in the back, betrayed.

She'd initially experienced a similar sharp stab of pain in her chest when she'd seen what Jesse was doing. But now . . .

"Something's wrong," she said quietly.

"Yeah, we've been robbed!" David announced.

"Why would he take the money?" she asked.

"Because he's an outlaw," David said as he closed his fingers around a fistful of bullets and dropped them into his pocket.

For pity's sake, how many times did he plan to shoot Jesse?

She shook her head. "But as far as I know he didn't need the money. He told me that when he participated in the bank robberies before, he kept only what he needed to survive." She flung her hand out in frustration. "He had everything he needed here: clothes, a roof over his head, food. He had no reason to steal from us. Why would he do this?"

"We'll ask him when we find him," her father said. "David, gather up the men."

"David, wait," Robert said. "I think Amelia's right."

"What makes you think so?" her father asked.

"That day we took him to Fort Worth, he said he didn't know how he'd pay us back. Why would he say that and then take from us? It makes no sense."

Her father looked at her. "You saw him ride out?"

She nodded mutely.

"Which way did he go?"

"North. Toward the line shack."

"Toward the Oklahoma territory," David said, his voice filled with impatience. "The longer we wait, the less likely we are to catch him."

Amelia sat up straighter in the chair. "The night he got caught robbing that bank . . . Papa, did you know that he'd stayed behind trying to stop that clerk from bleeding to death?"

Her father furrowed his brow deeply. "Judge Gray's notes didn't say anything about that. Who told you this?"

"Jesse told me tonight."

"He lied," David said.

"Why would he do that?" she asked. She looked at her father imploringly. "I'm afraid he must be in some kind of trouble."

"Of course he's in trouble, Amelia," David began. "He stole—"

"Will you stop?" she yelled, coming to her feet. "Will you stop thinking about *what* he did and try to help me figure out *why* he did it? You're loading your rifles and stuffing your pockets with bullets and he doesn't have a gun. He's not dangerous."

"But what if he is?" David asked.

"He's not," she assured him. "If he were, he would have hurt me when we went looking for that mustang a couple of hours ago."

Her father narrowed his eyes. "What are you talking about?"

"Jesse said he wanted to capture the mustang for me. We rode out to the ridge, and we talked. That's all we did." She felt heat burn her face. *Well, that and a little kissing.* "Something was bothering him. I thought it was the idea of capturing the mustang, but now I'm not so sure. Maybe he took the money because he didn't think he had a choice. Don't bring the men into the hunt. He'll just get killed if you do. They don't trust him any more than you do."

Her father nodded. "Perhaps you're right. We could begin the search. The men can follow an hour behind us. Then if we run into trouble at least we'll know they're coming after us. David, why don't you let Tanner know?"

As though the speaking of his name had summoned him, Tanner stepped into the library with Frank following in his wake.

"Judge, I think there's something you need to hear," Tanner said. He placed his hand on Frank's shoulder. "Go ahead and tell him."

Frank looked as though he wasn't as sure as Tanner was that he should speak. He licked his lips and shifted his feet.

"Come on, boy," her father barked. "We have important matters to see to."

Frank nodded as though he'd made his decision. "It's about Jesse and Mitch. It's no secret that Mitch has been planning to court Amelia. During the party when she went outside for a breath of air, Mitch followed her."

Amelia's stomach knotted up. Had Mitch spied on her?

Frank looked uncomfortable as he added, "He saw Amelia dance with Jesse. Saw him kiss her."

Amelia thought she might be ill. How dare Mitch spy on her!

Frank continued, "When Jesse headed back to the bunkhouse, Mitch followed far enough back that Jesse didn't know he was there. Mitch had planned to beat the ever-lovin' snot out of Jesse. Instead he overheard Jesse talking to some fella. Some fella named Pete."

"Sometimes-One-Eyed Pete?" Amelia asked, trepidation slicing through her.

"I don't know. I guess. Anyway, Mitch told me that he heard Jesse tell Pete that he'd get the money out of the safe and take it to Pete at the north line shack."

"Let's go," David ordered.

"Wait!" Amelia cried. David staggered to a stop. She met Frank's gaze. "Do you have any idea why Jesse would do this for Pete?"

Frank glanced around the room. "I think it had to do with you. Mitch said Pete threatened to hurt you if Jesse didn't do what he wanted."

"Why didn't Mitch come and tell us as soon as he heard all this?" Robert asked.

"I think Mitch figured you could protect Amelia. And

if Jesse took the money, you'd capture him, send him back to prison, and that would leave the way clear for Mitch to court Amelia. It's pretty obvious where Amelia's heart lies, and it's not with Mitch."

"All right. I'll deal with Mitch when we get back," her father said. "Tanner, you keep the men tethered here while my sons and I head to the line shack."

With an authoritative voice she'd never before used when speaking to her father, she announced, "I'm riding with you."

"No, you're not," her father said.

Amelia stepped toward her father. "Papa, I'm going. I can ride with you or I can follow behind you, but either way I'm going. I'm not your little girl anymore. I've grown up."

Sadness touched her father's eyes, then pride as he gave her an understanding smile. "I reckon you have at that."

CHAPTER TWENTY

With dawn easing over the horizon, Jesse drew his horse to a halt in front of the line shack.

Pete was sitting on the porch. He slowly came to his feet, stroking the gun tucked into the belt at his waist. Pete never had been one for wearing a holster. But he was quick to draw and quick to fire.

Jesse glanced around. Trees circled the clearing in front of the shack, making it possible for men to hide from sight if needed.

"Where's the rest of the gang?" Jesse asked.

"Still in Fort Worth, waiting on orders from me," Pete said.

Jesse dismounted and tossed the saddlebag to Pete. "That's all that was in the safe. I guess Judge Harper isn't as wealthy as everyone thinks."

Although he suspected the judge kept his money in a bank or two in Fort Worth.

Pete folded back the flap on the saddlebag and brought out a bundle of cash. "How much do you reckon is here?"

"I didn't take the time to count it. Maybe five hundred."

Pete rubbed his bristly chin. "That's not a bad start."

"What do you mean by that? It's not the start; it's the finish," Jesse told him. "Take the money, ride out of here, and don't look back. And if you ever threaten to hurt Amelia again, I'll deliver a bullet to you instead of money."

Although he didn't know how he was going to protect her when he was in prison.

"Tough talk for such a young fella. You never talked back to me before," Pete pointed out.

"I'm not a kid anymore, Pete."

"That's the gosh-darned truth if I ever heard it. Reckon you'll be an even greater asset to me now than you were before. Let's ride."

Pete ambled toward his horse.

"I'm not going with you, Pete."

Pete stopped as though he'd run smack-dab into a brick wall. He turned around. "Figurin' to head out on your own and start your own gang, huh? Just desert me like I was never nothin' to you."

Jesse slowly shook his head. "Nope. I figure I'm going back to prison. Amelia saw me take the money from the safe. I asked her to give me a two-hour head start. But I don't think she'll do that. She has too much respect for the law."

"Then we need to ride, boy! Ride now!"

"The two hours is my gift to you, Pete. I never planned to run."

"They'll send you back to prison, you idiot!" Pete yelled.

"I know. I'll serve out my remaining five years there . . . and then some." He figured they'd add on a few years for the robbery he'd committed today.

"Are you tellin' me that you're plannin' to just sit here and wait for them to capture you?" Pete asked.

"Yep. I just want to serve out my time and get on with my life. I don't want that life to be about taking what I haven't earned."

"You're talkin' crazy now," Pete said.

Maybe he was. Maybe he was foolish to turn himself in knowing that he'd go back to prison, knowing that he'd lost whatever affection Amelia had for him, knowing she wouldn't be here waiting on him when he got out.

But being with her had given him a glimpse of what life could be: a hint of love, trust, respect. Maybe in time he could experience it again.

"You'd best get to riding, Pete," Jesse said solemnly.

"Afraid it's a little too late for that," a voice boomed.

Jesse spun around. Judge Harper strode out from between the trees.

"Surrender," Judge Harper demanded. "You're surrounded."

Out of the corner of his eye, Jesse saw Pete quickly draw his gun.

"No!" Jesse cried.

He leaped between Pete and the judge.

Explosions ricocheted around him.

Agonizing fire tore through him.

Inky blackness engulfed him.

Jesse swam through the darkness.

It hurt to breathe. He thought he might have another busted rib. But the pain was lower. His side. His side ached.

He felt a warm, damp cloth on his face, his neck, his chest. Soothing. Incredibly soothing.

He heard a soft voice calling his name. Calling him from the abyss.

Slowly he opened his eyes.

Amelia smiled at him.

Amelia.

He'd never in his life known such gladness. Even though he'd be going back to prison, she was safe.

That was all that mattered.

That and the judge.

"Your father?" he rasped.

"He's all right." She combed the hair off his brow. "Thanks to you. You put yourself between him and Pete, took the bullet that was meant for him."

She made it sound as though he were some sort of hero. He shook his head. "Pete?"

"My brothers shot him. They were waiting behind the trees, and they didn't know how else to stop him. He died. I'm sorry, Jesse."

He was surprised by the sadness that engulfed him. He supposed that in a way Pete had been the father he'd never had.

He was in a room he didn't recognize. But it smelled like flowers. He had to be in a bedroom somewhere in the judge's house. Soon they'd be carting him to prison.

Before he went, he wanted to touch Amelia's face. Kiss her lips. Hold her as though there were no tomorrow.

But she would have other tomorrows.

So would he. But they'd be spent in prison.

And he didn't want to go without Amelia knowing the reason he'd done what he had.

"He planned to hurt you," he said quietly. "Kidnap you and make your father pay to get you back."

He wanted to touch her so badly that it almost hurt as much as the wound in his side. He could feel the bandage wrapped around him. They must have brought in a doctor while he'd been unconscious.

"We know. Mitch overheard you talking to him. That's the reason my brothers and I went with Papa—"

"You were there?" he interrupted.

"Yes."

"You could have gotten hurt or killed."

"I know, but I didn't want you to have to face my angry brothers alone."

She'd been there for him, worrying about him. Reaching out, he touched her cheek. So soft. He wanted that softness always.

He heard the sound of a throat being cleared, dropped his hand to the bed, and slammed his eyes closed. He hadn't realized someone else was in the room.

The judge.

Resounding footsteps echoed around the room. Jesse opened his eyes. Judge Harper stood at the foot of the bed, his arms crossed over his chest. His sons stood on either side of him.

"You know, Jesse, you could have saved us all a lot of trouble if you'd told us about your midnight meeting with Pete last night," Judge Harper said.

"Pete said if I told you, he'd hurt Amelia," Jesse told him.

Judge Harper nodded. "You seem to have a habit of trying to save people. Amelia told me what happened that night in the bank when you were captured. I've got some friends in high places. I'm going to have your case reopened."

"Are you going to have that clerk testify to what Jesse did?" David asked.

The judge shook his head. "No need. If Jesse says

he stayed behind and tried to stop the bleeding, that's good enough for me."

"You're taking my word on it?" Jesse asked.

"Is there some reason I shouldn't?" Judge Harper asked.

Jesse shook his head. "No, sir."

"Then I can pretty much guarantee that your sentence is going to be reduced to years already served. The next time you walk out of my house, Jesse Lawton, you'll do it as a free man."

Years already served. Free man.

Jesse could hardly believe what he was hearing. And he certainly didn't know what to say.

Amelia smiled with tears welling in her eyes as she squeezed his hand.

"Leave or stay, Jesse. The choice will be yours," Judge Harper said.

"I'm hoping you'll stay," Robert said. "I want to expand our operation to include horse breeding and training. I'd like you to be in charge of running things."

Amelia locked her gaze on Jesse's with everything she felt for him reflected in her eyes. She'd captured his heart, and in so doing, she'd freed him long before the judge had.

He smiled, hoping she could see in his face what she meant to him.

"Think I'll stay."

* * *

With a half dozen cowboys riding with him, Jesse guided the herd of untamed mustangs into the waiting corral.

In the past month, Jesse's life had changed in ways he'd never imagined. He'd fixed up the north line shack and was living there now.

Every evening he ate supper at the judge's table, discussing the day with Amelia and her family. Following the meal they'd all go to the parlor, where Amelia would read from her latest dime novel.

Jesse thought it was funny when Amelia would close the book after her reading and Judge Harper would urge her to read just one more chapter aloud.

He'd worried that the remaining members of the Nightriders gang might decide to follow through on Pete's plan and abduct Amelia. When he'd expressed his concerns to Judge Harper, he'd learned that there were no other members. The gang had disbanded long ago, while he'd been in prison. Pete had lied to him about there being others. Lied to manipulate him. It saddened him sometimes when he thought about Pete.

He turned his mind from the past back to the present.

One of the men closed the gate to the corral, and the horses pranced around the enclosure. Jesse would give them a few days to adjust to their new surroundings before he'd begin the arduous task of taming them.

He saw Mitch saunter out of the barn. The judge had kept him on, but his chores had been reduced to mucking out stalls and every other unpleasant task that could be found.

Jesse dismounted.

"I'll see to your horse," Frank said as he took the reins.

"Thanks." Jesse couldn't quite get used to the friendliness of the ranch hands.

He watched as Frank skirted widely around Mitch on his way into the barn. Mitch was now the one separated from the group, balancing at the edge. He was no longer the confident, cocky cowboy he'd once been. Now he looked as though he hoped no one would notice him.

Jesse understood that feeling too well. He strode over to Mitch.

"I need another hand to help me train the horses," Jesse said. "I was wondering if you wanted the job."

Mitch looked at him suspiciously. "Why offer it to me after what I did, hoping that you'd get sent back to prison?"

"It's like Tanner says. Every man deserves a second chance. You want the job or not?"

"How are you going to convince the judge and the others to let me do it?" Mitch asked.

"I don't have to convince them. I just have to tell

them that it's what I think is best. They'll trust my judgment on the matter."

Mitch nodded. "Reckon you earned that trust."

"Takes a while to earn trust back, but it can be done," Jesse assured him.

Mitch released a deep breath. "Yep, I'd like to work with the horses."

Jesse held out his hand. Mitch hesitated before giving it a firm shake.

"You can report to me in the morning," Jesse said with the confidence he was feeling these days. He knew his place, knew he belonged.

Turning, he caught sight of Amelia walking toward him. Seeing her, with a smile of welcome blossoming over her face, was his favorite part of the day.

Her father and brothers trailed behind her.

When she got near enough, she said, "I didn't think you wanted to capture the mustang."

"That was before you taught me how good it feels to have a place to come home to."

"I love you, Jesse."

His chest felt as though it might cave in on him. Or expand to touch the sky. He didn't know which.

"No one ever has," he said quietly.

She brushed her lips over his. "Well, I do, Jesse Lawton."

Right there beside the corral, in front of her father

and her brothers and the whole wide world, Jesse took her in his arms and kissed her with all the love he felt inside him.

He might have once been an outlaw, but Amelia Harper had stolen his heart.

DEAR READER:

Jesse seems like such a bad boy, but he's really just had a rough time of it and Amelia's not the good girl she appears to be. They're so perfect together that it's a good thing they found each other!

In Beverly Jenkins's JOSEPHINE AND THE SOLDIER, Adam Morgan may be a young Civil War hero, but that doesn't mean Jo isn't suspicious of him. She's known him since she was in pigtails, and she knows what a café au lait Casanova he is. What she doesn't realize is that when he turns his legendary charm her way, all her intentions of staying independent and beau-free seem to fly right out the window.

Turn the page to see them meet up for the first time in five years and watch the sparks fly!

Abby McAden
Editor, Avon True Romance

FROM
JOSEPHINE AND THE SOLDIER
by Beverly Jenkins

Jo hurried out to the wagon and after a short search found the scissors beneath the wagon seat. After hopping back down to the ground, her intent was to head back to her mother but Jo stood there a moment to enjoy the silence and the gentle June breeze. She looked out over the fields toward the horizon and drank in the lush green countryside. Michigan was so lovely in the spring, Jo could never imagine living anywhere else.

She was just about to head back when the sight of a rented hack pulling up to the front of the house made her stop. The driver, a short, gnarly old man, hurried around to open the door. Out stepped a light-skinned man on crutches. One leg was heavily bandaged from his knee to his toes, so Jo assumed him to be another veteran coming to stay with Mrs. Oswald. He hopped around a bit to get himself steadied, then said something to the driver. Jo watched the driver firmly drop a valise at the feet of the crutch-bearing man. The men spoke for a moment. Their voices rose. She was too far away to hear the entire argument, but it seemed the man on the crutches wanted the driver to carry the bag to the door, but the tight-jawed driver climbed back into his rig and drove away. The man didn't appear able to pick up the valise and handle the crutches, too, so she went to his aid.

As Jo neared, however, she realized that she knew him. Although she hadn't seen him since she was twelve, Jo was ready to bet every hair iron she owned that the golden-skinned man with the golden brown eyes was her brother's friend Adam Morgan. Happiness and surprise filled her. What was he doing here?

"Hello, Beautiful."

Jo stopped, then stared up into the handsome sculpted face of Adam Morgan. *Beautiful?!* When she was younger, her brother and his friends called her nothing but "Pest."

Adam regained her attention by adding, "I lived in Whittaker for ten years. I don't remember ever seeing you back then."

Jo blinked. He didn't recognize her?! She almost burst into laughter but decided to play along. She'd tease him later. "I've lived here all of my life."

"Really? I would remember someone as lovely as you."

"I bet you say that to all of the girls."

He clutched his heart. "You wound me, *mademoiselle*. Weren't the Rebs enough?"

Jo giggled in spite of herself. He was as silly as ever. He then introduced himself. "I'm Adam Morgan."

"Pleased to meet you, Adam."

Silence.

"Now you're supposed to give me your name," he pointed out.

Jo replied with sparkling eyes, "I don't think I will."

"Ah, a woman of mystery. I like intrigue."

"Do you?"

His voice softened. "I do."

Jo felt something come over her that she'd never felt before. George made her flutter, but this feeling was deeper, stronger somehow. It was like comparing the wind from the wings of a butterfly to that from the mighty wings of a red-tailed hawk.

"How old are you?" he asked.

It took Jo a moment to answer. "Seventeen."

"You've a mama nearby, I'm betting?"

Jo nodded. "Yes."

"Does she let you have dinner with soldiers?"

"No."

"Smart woman," he offered in tandem with his heart-melting smile.

As an adolescent, Jojo never understood why girls swooned every time Adam or his brother, Jeremiah, walked by. Now she did. Shaking herself free of his spell, she said, "I came to help you with your bag."

"Thanks."

Jo picked up the valise. It was heavy, but not so much

so that she couldn't lug it the short distance to the porch.
When they reached the door, Jo set it down. "I'll go and
find Mrs. Oswald for you."

His eyes were all she could see. She seemed to be
drowning in them. It was an oddly pleasant feeling. Then
remembering that this was Adam Morgan, she shook herself free again. "Nice meeting you, Adam."

"Nice meeting you as well, Beautiful. You aren't going
to tell me your name." It was a statement, not a question.

Jo smile secretively. "No, but I'm certain you'll learn it
soon."

Trudy had apparently come looking for Jo, because
she suddenly appeared at Jo's side. Jo sensed Trudy was
about to say something, but upon seeing the man Jo was
talking with, Trudy offered nothing but a look of utter
surprise. Jo assumed Trudy recognized him, too. He
didn't seem to recognize Trudy though, if the polite but
distant nod he sent her way was any indication. Jo supposed she and Trudy did look different from the short,
skinny, ringlet-wearing adolescents they'd been the last
time Adam had seem them. They were both taller, and
no longer skinny. Trudy was a bit rounder than Jo, but
they were young women now.

Before Trudy could open her mouth and ruin Jo's
game, Jo told Adam, "You go on inside and take a seat.
I'll fetch Mrs. Oswald. That is who you're here to see?"

"Yes, the hospital in Detroit recommended I stay

here until I recover." But he seemed more intent upon Jo, and she could feel the interest as well as she could feel the breeze on her cheeks. She grabbed the still-staring Trudy's arm. "Come on. Let's get Mrs. Oswald."

Once they got around to the back of the house, Trudy finally found her voice, "Jojo, that was Adam Morgan!"

"I know."

Trudy then gushed, "Lord, did you ever see anyone so handsome?"

Jo had to admit she had not. "He doesn't recognize either of us, though. He called me beautiful."

Trudy stopped dead in her tracks. "He did?"

"Yes." And as Jo recalled the incident now, she could still feel her insides shimmering like sun on the lake.

Jo and Trudy found Mrs. Oswald. She'd joined Cecilia, Belle, and the other women sewing beneath the trees. Before Jo could say a word, Trudy announced quickly, "Mrs. Best, Adam Morgan is here!"

Cecilia and Belle sat up in surprise.

Trudy added, "He didn't recognize us. He called Jojo beautiful!"

Jo wanted to bop her friend in the head for revealing that, but nothing could be done about it now.

Cecilia echoed skeptically, "Beautiful?"

Jo waved her hand dismissively. "Mama, you remember how Adam and Jere were? No female was safe from their silver tongues. Well, apparently, nothing's changed. Trudy's right about him not recognizing us, though. He didn't."

Cecilia smiled. "Adam and Jere were handfuls. Always respectful, but they lived for turning a young lady's head. Won't he be surprised when he finds out who you two really are!"

Once he did, Jo doubted he'd call her beautiful again, and for some reason that knowledge didn't sit real well with her. Jo, however, thought it wise not to put any stock in whatever Adam had to say. She'd seen the Morgan brothers work their magic on young ladies for many years, and she personally had no desire to be put through her paces by a café au lait Casanova. Besides, she was supposed to be starting up with George. She wondered where he'd gotten to. She glanced around the grounds and saw that he was still engrossed in his chess game.

Mrs. Oswald rose to her feet, saying, "I should go and meet the young man and assign him a space."

Cecilia and Belle got up as well.

"You know, Patricia, I loved those Morgan boys as if they were my own," Cecilia said to Mrs. Oswald. "Depending on how long Adam's going to stay and what his plans are, I'd be willing to take him into my home. We've the room. Haven't we, ladies?"

Belle nodded enthusiastically. Jo wasn't so sure about having the blarney-filled Adam Morgan under her roof.

Cecilia studied Jojo for a silent moment, but Jo responded with a smile she hoped would allay any concerns. "That might be nice, Mama."

Cecilia nodded. "Good. Then let's go and see him."